"I won't be blackmailed into sleeping with you!"

Cade was very much the gentleman of leisure as he knotted his tie and put on his jacket with swift, sure hands. "There is no deadline. You have plenty of time to change your mind."

"I won't!"

He raised a doubting eyebrow. "Don't you ever wonder, Lesley, whether the world really does rock when we make love? Aren't you the tiniest bit curious?"

"No, not if..."

He seemed to read her mind. "I'm not trying to blackmail you. I've already decided what I'm going to do with your bad check. I think I'll give it to your fiancé—as a wedding present. If you don't want him to have it, don't marry him."

He tipped an imaginary hat and closed the door behind him.

very good

Books by Leigh Michaels

HARLEQUIN PRESENTS
702—KISS YESTERDAY GOODBYE
811—DEADLINE FOR LOVE

HARLEQUIN ROMANCE
2657—ON SEPTEMBER HILL

These books may be available at your local bookseller.

Don't miss any of our special offers. Write to us at the following address for information on our newest releases.

Harlequin Reader Service
P.O. Box 52040, Phoenix, AZ 85072-2040
Canadian address: P.O. Box 2800, Postal Station A,
5170 Yonge St., Willowdale, Ont. M2N 6J3

LEIGH MICHAELS

deadline for love

Harlequin Books

TORONTO • NEW YORK • LONDON
AMSTERDAM • PARIS • SYDNEY • HAMBURG
STOCKHOLM • ATHENS • TOKYO • MILAN

Harlequin Presents first edition August 1985
ISBN 0-373-10811-7

Original hardcover edition published in 1985
by Mills & Boon Limited

CHAPTER ONE

SHE was tall, slender as a willow, and elegant in the tailored blazer and high-waisted trousers. The emerald green suit was intended for travelling, and it gave no hint that the young woman who looked so fashionable had just spent the night in a coach seat on Amtrak's California Zephyr because no sleeping compartments were available on the train.

As Lesley Allen walked through Chicago's Union Station, more than one man paused to get a better look, wondering if she was a top-fashion model; her walk had that sort of grace, and her colouring, with silky black hair curling around her heart-shaped face and big green eyes fringed by dark lashes, was just as striking. Several would have liked to do more than look, but Lesley didn't notice. And though her stride didn't appear to be hurried, even the porter had trouble keeping up with her on her way to the cab stand.

He sighed in relief as he shepherded her monogrammed two-suiter and the matching leather travel case into the cab and pocketed his tip.

'The Metro Tower on North Michigan,' Lesley told the cabbie, and the vehicle screeched out of the underground loading area and into the bustling traffic of the Loop.

Lesley leaned forward to watch Chicago speed by, and was nearly thrown on to the floor as the cabbie braked for a red light. Four days out of the city and she missed it; she had to readjust her brain with an almost audible click to the frantic pace.

The streets looked ghostly today, wrapped in heavy blankets of fog. Only the bottom twenty stories of the Sears Tower were visible; the building looked as if it had been sheered off. No wonder O'Hare was fog-

bound, she thought, and was glad that she had taken
the train. She didn't trust instrument flying; she much
preferred seeing where she was going. Besides, she could
now write a feature for the magazine about the future
of American rail service.

But the heavy air didn't change the pace at street
level. The traffic light turned green and inertia pressed
her into the seat as the cabbie floored the accelerator.
They don't need all that fancy equipment to train
astronauts, Lesley mused. Just let them ride with a
Chicago cabbie, and they'd know what to expect on lift
off.

The cab made a sharp turn on to Michigan Avenue
and crossed the river. Lesley mapped their progress past
the Wrigley Building, its brass doors and window
frames gleaming even though there was no sunlight
today to reflect from them; past the old Chicago Water
Tower, one of the few survivors of the great fire that
had levelled most of the city. She wanted to throw her
arms out and embrace Chicago; it felt so good to be
home.

The cab swerved to the kerb in front of the Metro
Tower and Lesley gathered up handbag, travel bag and
two-suiter and slid out. She stood for a moment on the
sidewalk, staring straight up the smoke-coloured glass
wall of the Tower to where the fog hovered, concealing
the top two-thirds of the building. This is where I
belong, she thought. This is the centre of my universe.

The cabbie leaned out of his window. 'Hey, Lady!' he
yelled plaintively. 'Are you a tourist or what? The fare,
lady—pay the fare!'

Lesley pulled a bill from her blazer pocket and thrust
it into his hand. He was still shaking his head and
muttering invectives as the cab growled into gear and
sped off, belching black smoke as it darted into the
beginnings of rush-hour traffic.

Lesley glanced at the tiny diamond-studded watch
that hung from a gold chain around her neck, and
smiled at the businessman who gave the revolving door

a push for her. But it was a cool, abstracted smile that gave him no encouragement to speak.

She stopped at the condominium office, and the smiling receptionist handed her a fat plastic bag. 'I'm glad you're home, Miss Allen,' she said. 'Your mailbox had been crammed.'

Lesley returned the smile. 'I'm always the most popular when I'm out of town,' she said.

The same businessman held the elevator for her and tried to start a conversation. Lesley answered in cool, polite monosyllables and revised her plans. If she went on up to her condo, he might follow. She'd stop at the office first instead.

On the thirtieth floor she was greeted by a six-foot-high reproduction of the cover of last month's *Today's Woman* magazine. The cover girl really was delicious, Lesley mused. They would use her again. A woman who was still beautiful under twenty-power magnification was hard to find.

Beyond the plate-glass door, the office was bustling. She stood in the doorway a second, drinking in the flavour of her little empire. Then she waved at the receptionist, who was on the telephone.

The girl said something into the receiver and pushed the hold button. 'It's Jay Nichols,' she told Lesley. 'Shall I have him hold?'

'Did you tell him I was here?'

'No. I just said I'd check to see if you'd come in yet.'

'I'll call him back. I want to look through my messages, at least.' Behind the small reception area lay the big single office, filled with desks, that was the brain of the magazine. It was getting crowded, Lesley thought; they needed more space. She'd have to talk to Jay about it.

The two-suiter was getting heavy as she crossed the big, well-lit room to her own tiny glass-walled office. She'd learned years ago to travel light, but even that had been too much this time.

She stopped at her door and childishly traced the

nameplate with a slim finger. The sight of that engraved brass plate saying 'Lesley Allen, Editor' still brought a light of triumph to her eyes. Not many women under the age of thirty could claim the title. In fact, most of the women's magazines in the country were still edited by men. It was a remnant of the Dark Ages, Lesley thought.

Her smile as she studied the plaque would have amazed any of the men who had paused that day to take a second look. Her green eyes glowed, and a dimple peeked out at the corner of her mouth. It had been years since any man had seen that smile.

Shelah Evans, the assistant editor, came out of the office next to Lesley's and dropped a folder on their secretary's desk. 'Boy, am I glad you're back,' she said. She took the two-suiter out of Lesley's hand and followed her into the inner office, a pile of message slips in the other hand.

Lesley flexed her fingers in relief and stowed the bags in her closet. 'Why? What's going on?'

'Check the in-basket and you'll see.'

A look at the overflowing tray on the corner of her desk made Lesley wince. She slid out of the emerald blazer and hung it up, ran a comb through the artfully tangled curls that wisped around her face, and straightened the neckline of the pastel green blouse.

'Where's Jana?' she asked.

'Your beloved secretary called in sick and dumped the whole mess on me. Do you want me to start from the beginning, or work backward?'

'Just give me today's problems,' Lesley said. 'If the other stuff has lasted all week, it will keep till tomorrow when she's back.'

'You're the boss.' Shelah crossed one elegant leg over the other and opened the notebook. 'How was our famous movie star, by the way?'

Lesley shrugged. 'He still thinks he's Tom Selleck and Burt Reynolds wrapped up in one handy package. He chased me around the house the first two days I was there.'

'Did you get the interview?'

'Do I ever come back without one? And much as I'd like to tear him to shreds, he'll look great in print. Which reminds me . . .' She pulled a film pouch—lead-lined to protect the precious film from airport X-rays—out of her handbag.

Shelah reached for it. 'I'll send it to the lab first thing. Rush?'

'Of course. We're working against deadline with this one. I think I got some really good shots of him.' Lesley was sorting the mail on her desk. 'I just pretended I was looking through the sights of a gun.'

'The readers will love it. But what a waste, Lesley. A week with Derek Stone—You should have come back with a dreamy smile, ready to write about what a marvellous lover he is.'

Lesley looked up in surprise. 'How would I know whether he's a marvellous lover?'

'That's just it, Lesley. Why don't you know? You're a liberated, career woman, with nothing to lose, and I'll bet that he was willing.'

'Shelah, are we going to get to my messages eventually?'

'I would have been in his bed before he knew what hit him. And then I'd have asked some really interesting questions. The readers would love to know the real reasons why Marissa Benton divorced him.'

'If that's what you want to know, call Marissa Benton.'

'I just might do that.'

'Besides, Shelah, if he was such a terrific lover, you probably couldn't have remembered your name. That's why you stayed here, and I interviewed Derek Stone.'

'All right. If you insist that men are unnecessary . . .'

'I don't. Remember? I'm engaged to Jay Nichols.' Lesley waved her left hand, with its full-carat marquise diamond, set in antique gold, under Shelah's nose.

'You've been engaged for two years. If you loved the man, you couldn't stand not to sleep with him.'

'How would you know whether I'm sleeping with Jay?'

Shelah gave her a knowing, almost pitying, smile. 'Because Jay is too conventional. And he's almost fifty, Lesley.'

'Forty-six is not almost fifty, Shelah!' Lesley snapped. 'My messages, if you please?'

'All right, all right,' Shelah muttered and opened the notebook. 'Today's list, from the top—Jay called. Your favourite advice columnist called and wants her salary doubled or she's quitting. That paediatrician out at the children's hospital is intrigued by the idea of a monthly column and wants to have lunch with you. Jay called. The premier manufacturer of disposable diapers is not happy with the comparison study in last month's issue and is threatening to pull his advertising. Jay called. The shipment of appliances that we're supposed to test for the next issue is stranded on a rail siding by a truckers' strike. Jay called. The chairperson of one of the women's lib groups wants to know when you're going to let your readers know that there is more to life than dishwashers and babies . . .' She paused for a breath.

'Is that all?' Lesley asked dryly.

'No. And Jay called. That's just today, of course.'

'Have Jana check my calendar for next week and set them all up for lunch. The paediatrician can come to the staff dining room here. I'll take the diaper man to the Ninety-Fifth—that might impress him. And tell the advice columnist to bring an egg-salad sandwich in her own brown bag.'

'Where do you want to take Jay?' Shelah grinned. 'And do you want all the truckers that are on strike? You did say lunch for everyone.'

Lesley didn't look up. 'See if you can persuade the shipping company to do a little extra work. And I'll call Jay. Why don't you try for a little respect? The man does still own this magazine, after all.'

'But not for long, thank God. We might even come

up with an owner who believes in putting some of the profits back into the *Woman.*'

Lesley frowned. 'Or one who believes in total editorial control. Jay's not bad, in comparison.'

'You like it when he leaves everything to you. When are you going to stop living and breathing this magazine and start enjoying yourself?'

'Out, Shelah. I have work to do.'

Shelah's voice turned suddenly serious. 'You're so busy only because you think you have to write fifty percent of every issue. Why don't you delegate some of the work?'

Lesley looked up with a smile, the dimple peeking out again. 'All right. Practice your top management skills and fire the advice columnist. And then you can take her place for a few months. We'll see how you do.'

'I was thinking more in terms of the paediatrician, Lesley.' The tone was confiding.

'You hate kids, Shelah.'

'But he has such a dreamy voice . . .' Shelah floated off to her own office.

Lesley reflected that if Shelah was really as dizzy as she sounded, she'd have been fired long ago. But underneath the fluffy-blonde act, the girl was sharp—a good writer and an incisive editor. Now if she'd just stop chasing every man who came into her vicinity . . . She might make a good advice columnist, though; there was scarcely a male-female situation that Shelah hadn't experienced.

Lesley pulled a sheaf of yellow legal paper out of her handbag and reached for a pen to make corrections on the first draft of the Stone interview. Jana could type it in the morning, and then Lesley could work it over. It would be close to deadline, but she could make it. Too bad Amtrak didn't provide typewriters, or the article would be done by now.

Derek Stone. She sat still, thinking about Derek Stone and men like him—men who thought that a woman was a plaything, who refused to believe that she

had any value outside the bedroom. No doubt, she
thought, that attitude accounted for his divorce.

Lesley had learned early, and hard, about men like
Derek Stone. She'd like to write about what she saw;
she'd like to describe the way that Derek Stone's eyes
roved over a woman and the way that his brain almost
visibly calculated the precise amount of charm it would
take to get her into his bed. Well, it hadn't worked with
Lesley Allen. Derek Stone's charm had left her
unmoved.

And of course she wouldn't write it the way she
wanted. Her audience wasn't interested in the man's
flaws; they would read her prose and sigh as they
imagined themselves to be the woman to whom those
big blue eyes beckoned. It was fortunate for them,
Lesley thought, that they would probably never cross
Derek Stone's path. He, and men like him, consumed
women and tossed them aside, drained.

She glanced down at the legal pad, where her pen had
scribbled a vicious blot that cut through the paper. She
laughed at herself shakily. It wasn't fair to take it all
out on Derek Stone, she told herself. It wasn't his fault
that his attitude, even the tone of his voice, reminded
her of those rough lessons learned so long ago at the
hands of a man just like him.

She pushed the story into her desk drawer and dug
her luggage out of the closet. She was tired. A night's
sleep would do wonders.

'I'm going home,' she told Shelah, leaning around the
corner into the next office.

'To what? A cup of tea and a book? You don't even
have a cat to keep you company, for crying out loud.
Let's go out and shake up the town. I know a couple of
guys who . . .'

'I spent last night in a coach seat on a train. I'm in
no shape to carouse. See you tomorrow.' She didn't
bother to bring up Jay's name again; Shelah refused to
believe that Lesley's long-standing engagement meant
anything at all.

Her two-bedroom condo ten floors above the magazine office smelled musty from being shut up for nearly a week. She dropped her luggage in the foyer and turned up the thermostat. Autumn was here, and the stale air felt chilly. First stop, the kitchen, she decided, so she could put the kettle on. Darn Shelah, anyhow—a cup of tea sounded good.

As it always did, coming back to the condo gave her a sense of pride, of achievement. Not bad for a kid from the boondocks, she thought, looking around. The little country kitchen with its stained-glass cabinet doors, the tiny second bedroom that she had fixed up as a writing room with white wicker and green plants, the big balcony bedroom with the wrought-iron spiral staircase—she had always wanted spiral stairs. It felt good to know that it was hers—the labour of her own hands.

She dumped the bag of mail on the counter and turned the envelopes over as she waited for the water to boil. A big manila envelope caught her attention, and with trembling hands she tore it open. If it was another rejection slip, she thought, she would not be able to stand the pain.

Twenty pages of carefully typed manuscript slid into her hands—the first section of the book she was working on. And on top of it was a letter—not a printed rejection slip, but a personal letter.

She scanned it in a frenzy, picking up phrases. 'Might be made suitable for publication . . . at present, too dry and factual . . . try for a more personal approach to the subject . . . your credentials are excellent . . .'

Lesley laughed at that. Just how much better could credentials be? she wondered. The water boiled, and she made her tea. Then she carried the mug into the living room and curled up with the first twenty pages of her book.

Half an hour later she put it aside and dumped the cold tea down the kitchen drain. It was worth a try, she thought. The editor must know his business, and if he said it needed a more personal touch, perhaps he was right. She'd have a quick supper and then she'd start in again, from a whole new approach, Already sentences were beginning to form in her head.

The telephone shrilled, and Lesley jumped. Damn, she thought, it was probably Jay. She'd completely forgotten to call him back.

'Angel,' he said, and there was a thread of relief in his soft voice. 'I'm glad you're home safe.'

'Jay, I'm sorry I didn't return your call. My desk was buried in work and I forgot.'

There was no reproach in Jay Nichols' soft voice. 'It's all right, Angel, I know that you're busy. You haven't forgotten that we're having cocktails with Mother tonight, have you?'

Lesley groaned. 'Oh, Jay, I forgot. She'll just have to excuse me.'

'She won't like it, dear. And she's just now beginning to accept the idea of us being married.'

'But I'm exhausted, and I was going to ...' She sighed. 'All right, Jay. I'll get dressed.'

She could almost see his sweet smile. 'You're a trooper, Angel. I'll pick you up in half an hour, so we won't be too late. You can be ready by then, can't you?'

Lesley sighed and stuffed the manuscript back into the envelope. Maybe someday I can finish it, she thought. 'I'll be ready.'

She wished her bedroom had a door to slam; it would have helped to lessen her frustration. She could cheerfully consign Jay's mother to the pit of hell tonight. As exhausted as she was, there was nothing that she wanted less than to be exposed to Emily Nichols' saccharine sarcasm. But she knew that if she didn't go to the cocktail party, all the hard-won concessions the old lady had made over the past two years would be gone, and Lesley would be back at the beginning. For months Emily had referred to Lesley as 'That Woman who has her claws into poor, dear Jay.' Lesley wasn't about to start at the beginning again.

She was dressed before the deadline, though she was

still using a curling brush on her hair when the doorbell played its chastened version of Beethoven's Fifth. She put the brush down with a sigh and answered the door.

Jay was elegant in black dinner clothes, his salt-and-pepper hair neatly combed. She looked up into his eyes; Lesley was nearly as tall as he. He put a gentle kiss on her cheek, but looked a little doubtful as he studied her dress.

'Too much of a scarlet woman?' The dress had seemed a good idea when she bought it; the shimmer of brilliant red satin against her creamy skin and black hair could lift her spirits on the dullest of days. But the dress was practically strapless, and the slit up the side was no doubt far past what Emily Nichols would consider to be chaste. The matching red satin shoes were wickedly high-heeled.

'It's lovely on you. But I'm afraid Mother might . . .' Jay looked a little worried.

Suddenly Lesley was angry. Just when was Jay going to grow up and stop referring every judgment to his mother? She was certain of one thing, she decided. From now on she would dress to suit herself, and she would never again ask if Emily might be shocked by her choice of clothes.

'It's this outfit, or I'm staying home,' she said. 'There isn't time to change. And even if there was, everything else I own is at the cleaners.'

Jay glanced at his watch and nodded reluctant agreement. On the way to his mother's North Shore mansion, though, he was almost silent, and he kept looking over at Lesley with uncertainty in his eyes. It wasn't until Emily's butler had taken their coats that Jay spoke. 'Angel—we'll have to leave in an hour, I have dinner reservations.'

She nodded her agreement, thinking that she couldn't be more delighted. Usually these affairs dragged on for the entire evening and ended with them invited, with a show of reluctance, to dine with Emily, an invitation which Jay always accepted while Lesley seethed. She did care for Jay, but Emily!

'That's really why I wanted you to come. I'm negotiating a sale for the magazine.'

'Oh? Who's looking?' She tried to sound casual. She had tried for months to talk him out of selling the *Woman*, but it was one thing Jay was adamant about.

Jay smiled at her unconcerned tone and flicked a finger gently across her cheek. 'Don't pretend not to care, brat. You made your point about buyers—I'm being very selective. If Randall buys it, the *Woman* will be part of the biggest publishing empire in the country.'

'Cade Randall!' The name burst out despite her efforts to keep silent. 'Jay, you can't sell it to him!'

Jay frowned. 'Why not? The Randall Group is well-run, it's profitable . . .'

'And the whole corporation is based on that porno magazine!'

Jay shrugged. '*Monsieur* is Randall's biggest money-maker. But it isn't exactly pornography, Lesley.'

'Close enough,' Lesley muttered.

Jay looked confused. 'But you didn't want the *Woman* sold to anyone who wasn't involved with magazines. There just aren't many buyers around.'

'Why didn't you tell me you were talking to him about it?'

'I wanted to be certain he was interested before I got your hopes up. I assumed that you'd be delighted.'

'Well, you're wrong, Jay.'

A girl cooed at Lesley's side, 'Squabbling again? What a pair of lovebirds. Hi, Daddy. Grandmère is simply livid that you're late,' Kara Nichols tipped her cheek up for Jay's dutiful kiss. Then she added, with a frown, 'Hello, Lesley.'

Kara was sixteen, Lesley reminded herself. Of course a girl of that age didn't appreciate the idea of a stepmother still in her twenties. But that didn't excuse Kara's attitude. In the two weeks that Kara had been staying with her grandmother, Lesley had seen the girl several times. Kara was never quite rude, but the light in her eyes always made Lesley want to strangle her.

Jay was nervous. 'We'd better make sure Mother sees us right away,' he said. 'Do you want a glass of wine, Lesley?'

'No, thanks. As tired as I am, one glass and I'd fall asleep in the punchbowl. I'll just drink Perrier tonight.'

She waited a few yards from the bar while he got their drinks.

'Need a drink, Les?' A man in a checked sports jacket tapped her on the shoulder.

'No, thanks, Bob. Jay's getting me one.'

'Good for old Jay. When are you girls over at the magazine going to start running full-length novels every month? Everybody else is, and I've got some terrific stuff I'd like to offer you.'

Lesley smiled, and the dimple peeked out. 'Everybody else turned you down, right?'

'Lesley, how could you think that? You never come second with me.'

She turned serious. Bob Merrill was an authors' agent; perhaps he could help her. 'Bob, you handle a lot of writers, don't you? I mean, you're pretty well-known.'

He shrugged. 'I'm getting there, I guess. It puts the food on the table.'

'Would you give me some advice? I have a manuscript that's been rejected three times, and this time it came back with a letter suggesting that I've used the wrong approach. Should I rewrite it?'

His attention was obviously caught. 'A personal letter? From whom?' He whistled when she told him the name. 'Rewrite it, honey. The man knows his business, and if he took the time to write a letter ... This time, give it to me before you mail it. I'll only charge you five per cent of what you make.'

'Making me a special deal, hmm?'

Bob grinned. 'I'm having a half-price sale this week. I have to go prod one of my clients into writing a book—she's already spent the advance, so she owes them. Then I'm going to escape from this mausoleum and get something to eat. Are you and Jay staying around to dance attendance on his mama?'

'No. Jay has a business dinner. And Bob? Please don't say anything to Jay about the book. He doesn't know I'm writing it.'

'Me? Now why would I give away a client's secrets? See you later, Lesley. And think about putting a novel in the *Woman* one of these months!'

Just thinking about the magazine brought her back to the dinner appointment. She should have expected this to happen, she told herself. When Jay had first started talking about selling *Today's Woman*, she should have known that the Randall Group would come into it eventually. There were few magazine publishers who were making profits enough to consider purchasing another title, and Jay's price was high.

Lesley took a deep breath. There was no point in panicking, she told herself. The sale might fall through. And even if it didn't, she had other places to go. She didn't want to spend her life editing *Today's Woman*, anyway. If Cade Randall bought it, she'd find another job.

Another half-dozen deep breaths steadied her pulse, and she was able to smile at Jay when he put the icy glass of Perrier water into her hand.

'Am I forgiven?' he asked. 'Anyway, Lesley, that's one of the points we're arguing about. I'm insisting on it being written into the contract that the *Woman* remain structurally as it is.'

'No matter what he agrees to, if Cade Randall buys it, he'll change the rules,' Lesley said cynically. 'But I don't want to argue with you, Jay.'

'We'll talk about it later,' he promised. 'We'd better go see Mother.'

The biggest thrill of my evening, Lesley thought, but she put on her best smile as they approached the little dais where Emily Nichols sat. Her silver-blue hair was elaborately drawn up atop her head, and her grey silk dress was both brand-new and in the high kick of fashion twenty years ago.

Lesley gave her points. At least the woman knew that she would have looked ridiculous in today's clothes. Fashion, after all, should be what was becoming. It would be an interesting feature for the magazine, she thought—adapting the newest of fashion for women of all ages.

Kara was seated beside her grandmother, her red-shaded mouth pouty, her improbably blonde hair flowing around her shoulders. The girl looked as if she was playing at dressing-up, trying to look twenty instead of sixteen.

Emily said to the woman next to her, 'Isn't it marvellous that Joyce has let me borrow Kara for a little while? I can't imagine the child wanting to leave her mother to come back here, but her devotion to me is so very charming.'

'How is Joyce?' the other woman asked.

'Oh, she's all right. It nearly broke her heart to have to divorce Jay, of course, when he got involved with that woman, but she's recovering very well. Living in Paris helps a great deal, of course. She says she will never come back to Chicago as long as Jay and that woman are here.'

'The one who works for his magazine?'

'Yes. He says that he's going to marry her. I can't imagine what he's thinking about ... Hello, Jay dear.' She held her cheek up for his kiss. 'I thought you'd never arrive. And Lesley.' Her tone held a noticeable lack of enthusiasm, and her eyes snapped wide open as she surveyed the red satin dress.

Lesley was furious about the conversation they had overheard, but Jay didn't seem to notice. Damn it, she raged to herself, Emily knew perfectly well that she and Jay had never dated until after Joyce Nichols had moved to Paris. And she'd bet that Emily and Joyce had never been as intimate during the marriage as they seemed to be now. But Emily hated the idea of Jay marrying someone who didn't belong to her own social crowd, so she was helping to spread the rumour. And Jay did nothing to stop her.

She loved Jay, she told herself. She really did, but the same gentleness that made him so attractive to her kept him from standing up to Emily. Well, Lesley, you can't have both, she told herself. Emily is a small price to pay, after all, for having Jay.

CHAPTER TWO

'ANGEL, what is it that bothers you so much about the Randall Group buying the magazine?' Jay's question was soft and puzzled.

Lesley sighed and turned her head against the soft leather upholstery of the Mercedes. In the several years she had known him, Lesley reflected, she had never heard Jay raise his voice. He didn't have a temper, or at least she had never stumbled across it. 'I just don't like the idea of the *Woman* being associated with that flea-bitten rag Cade Randall calls a magazine.'

Amazingly, Jay laughed. 'Have you ever read *Monsieur*?'

'Not cover to cover, no. But enough to get the idea. Why sell the *Woman* now, Jay? It's making a profit. Let me run it for another couple of years.'

Jay shook his head. 'I can't, darling. I have to take money out of it this year to pay Joyce the rest of the divorce settlement. If I borrow against it, it can't turn a profit next year, and then it won't sell. It's simple economics, dear.'

It wasn't the first time that Lesley had cursed the idea of alimony. Middle-class women who needed it to support their children were having to throw their husbands in jail to make them pay up. Yet a woman like Joyce Nichols, who had inherited millions from her father, was able to force her ex-husband into liquidating his assets to give her money she would never need. Paris! What a joke.

'You know that the magazine never really interested me, anyway, Angel. I think it's a miracle that it's making money.'

Lesley bit her tongue. It was no miracle, she thought rebelliousiy, it was her hard work. But Jay was right about one thing—he had never expected to end up owning a magazine. How *Today's Woman* had found its way into the Nichols family at all was enough of a puzzle.

Jay found a spot to park his Mercedes and helped her out of the front seat. She tried one more time.

'Couldn't we just keep it, Jay? Why does it have to be sold at all? It will make a living for us. I can make it pay eventually, even if you have to borrow against it.'

'Do you think I want to be known around Chicago as the man whose wife supports him? No, Lesley.' It was the closest she had ever seen him come to losing his temper. 'If you want to freelance after we're married, fine. But I'm not going to live off your earnings. We'll sell the magazine, pay off Joyce, invest what's left in something safe, and we'll never have another care.'

She would have argued that point too, but the maitre d' was bowing them to a table. Jay didn't understand just how important the magazine was to her. If it couldn't be the *Woman*, then there would be another one in her future. There would have to be. The sticky four-colour ink of magazine publishing had crept into her veins long ago, and she could never be content if she was separated from it.

At least, she thought suddenly, Jay had accepted her reason for not wanting Cade Randall to buy the magazine. If he hadn't believed her, and had pressed for the truth . . .

Perhaps it wouldn't be Cade who joined them tonight for dinner, she realized. *Today's Woman* was a side dish compared to the rest of the Randall Group's holdings; Cade probably devoted his time to the main courses. *Monsieur*, for one.

Just thinking about that magazine made Lesley furious. At least, she assured herself, what she had told Jay was the truth. It just wasn't quite the whole truth.

'Sure you don't want a martini, Angel?' Jay's voice was back to its usual softness.

Lesley shook her head resolutely. 'Perrier,' she told the waiter. 'I want a clear head,' she told Jay.

He looked alarmed. 'Well, don't act as if you're going into battle. After all, the three of us are hoping for the same thing. Cade Randall wants the magazine, I want to get rid of it, and you want it to have a good owner.'

'I'm not sure they're all the same thing, Jay. By the way, Bob Merrill asked again when we're going to start running novels in the *Woman*. I'd like to. It would be a real boost to circulation if the readers got a full book along with their magazine.'

Jay shook his head. 'I know, Angel, but it would also mean an increase in cover price, because the *Woman* isn't big enough to absorb that cost lightly. Let's let the new ownership make the decisions on it.'

'Perhaps we could give the new owners more for their money, too,' Lesley argued.

'I thought perhaps you and Bob were talking about a different kind of book. Why don't you try writing one, Angel? You have the talent, and you might like it better than magazines.'

'Nothing is better than magazines, Jay.' She didn't want Jay to know about the book; if it was ever accepted there would be plenty of time to tell him. It would, after all, require a fair amount of explanation. But she'd worry about that if the book was ever published—if, in fact, she ever had time to finish writing it at all, she thought, a little sourly.

The maitre d' was back, holding the chair opposite her for a woman who wore the lowest cut evening gown Lesley had ever seen. It probably would have displayed her navel, Lesley thought, if the tablecloth hadn't been in the way.

She was blonde, and she was undeniably pretty under the heavy eye makeup. She giggled nervously as Jay, always the perfect gentleman, rose. 'Miss . . .'

'Oh, just call me Bambi,' she said, her voice breathless.

'Miss Bambi,' Jay murmured.

Oh, for heaven's sake, Lesley thought. What kind of woman would let herself be called Bambi? And what kind of woman had only one name?

Then she looked up at the man who was reaching for Jay's outstretched hand and answered her own question. The kind of woman Cade Randall slept with, of course.

'Cade, this is the young woman I told you about,' Jay was saying. 'She's made *Today's Woman* what it is. Lesley Allen.'

'Mrs Allen?' There was a smooth question in Cade Randall's voice as he grasped her hand firmly. His was strong and brown; her slim fingers felt lost in his grip.

'Miss,' she supplied stiffly and pulled her hand away. She was tingling all the way up to her elbow, and she tried to hide it as she sipped her drink.

He seated himself beside her, ordered a drink for Bambi without asking what she wanted, and then turned back to Lesley. 'Jay has told me some very interesting things about you.'

She wanted to snap at him that Jay didn't know any of the most interesting things about her, but as she looked into his velvety brown eyes, she was unable to see anything in their depths other than casual interest in a business acquaintance.

She drew a tiny shocked breath. Was it possible that he didn't remember?

And then she knew. Of course he didn't remember. Ten years ago, she had been just another girl with one name. What could there be after ten years to remind Cade Randall of a one-night-stand named Lesley?

Dinner jerked along, with Jay and Cade talking business, Lesley silent as much as possible, and Bambi interrupting now and then with comments so ingenuous that even Cade was beginning to look impatient. Of course, Lesley thought cattily, it was probably the first time he'd taken her anywhere except to bed. And from the look of things, poor Bambi would never get out of the bedroom again.

'Your name is very familiar,' Cade told Lesley suddenly.

She choked on her chocolate cheesecake.

'I've read the last few issues of the magazine, since Jay and I started talking about the sale. And it seems to me that your by-line shows up very frequently.'

Lesley closed her eyes for a split second and sent a thankful prayer skyward. 'I enjoy writing, Mr Randall. I like to find out about new things and then share that knowledge with my readers.'

Jay laughed. 'She can probably get six story ideas from this table that would appeal to the *Woman*'s readers.'

Cade's brown eyes rested on Lesley. 'Will you take the challenge, Miss Allen?'

She looked thoughtfully across the table. Her number one choice would be the effect of the sexual revolution on dumb blondes, but Jay would think she was deliberately harassing their guests. 'All right.' She tapped her demitasse cup. 'European coffees—what they really are and how to make them.'

Cade nodded. 'One.'

'Irish linen. How do you know when you see the real thing? This is one of the few restaurants that use it, by the way.'

He nodded again.

'The centrepiece gives me two—a feature on how to make unusual candles for gifts, and one on arranging your own flowers. If you count drying flowers separately, I can get three out of it.'

He shook his head. 'I'll count it as two.'

'Then I just need two more. The most obvious one is how to bone a chicken breast for Chicken Kiev, and . . .'

For the life of her she could not see a sixth idea. She sat silent for what seemed forever, then shook her head.

Jay started to smile. 'The last story is sitting next to you, Angel,' he said gently. 'The *Woman*'s readers would love to hear about Cade Randall.'

Cade smiled. 'I'll count it. Congratulations. But I'd like to see you do the same thing in another setting,

Miss Allen. Of course your readers are interested in food and crafts. But if you were to accept that challenge somewhere else . . .'

'In bed?' Bambi asked brightly.

There was a sparkle in Cade's big brown eyes, as if he wished he had said it himself.

Lesley hoped that she wasn't turning red. 'The women who read my magazine are just as interested in sex as in food and crafts,' she told Bambi as gently as she could. 'And they are only beginning to enjoy the freedom of the bedroom that men have for generations.'

'They are?' The blonde sounded disappointed.

'When do you liberated women find the time?' Cade murmured.

'Mr Randall,' Lesley said curtly, 'you obviously have both an active career and a consuming interest in sex. Why not allow a woman the same liberty?'

He smiled. 'I would like to talk about how you do your research,' he suggested silkily. 'You wrote an article a couple of months ago called *The Bedside Manner*, and it wasn't about doctors.' There was a challenge in his eyes.

Bambi had lost interest again. 'Cade, where's the little girl's room?'

Lesley reached for her tiny evening bag. 'I'll show you, Bambi. The directions are hard to follow.'

There was now no mistaking the glint of amusement in Cade's eyes. 'Running, Miss Allen?'

'We'll wait for you in the foyer, Angel.' Jay pushed his chair back. 'Then we can go straight to the dance floor.'

Bambi spent most of her time studying herself in the mirror, Lesley did a quick repair job on her lipstick and sank into one of the blue velvet chairs in the tiny lounge.

'You scared me at first, Miss Allen,' the girl giggled. 'I get real uptight around career girls. Usually I feel so dumb, because I just have a job, not a career or anything.'

'What do you do?' Instantly Lesley was sorry she had asked.

'Oh, I'm a receptionist. At least I was till this photographer found me. I was in *Monsieur* a couple of months ago.'

'That's where you met Mr Randall, of course.'

'Yeah. Cade's a real nice guy.'

'The answer to every maiden's prayer,' Lesley muttered.

'What?' Bambi was confused, but when Lesley didn't offer to explain, she let it drop. 'Now I think I'll be a model. I've had several offers.'

I'll just bet you have, Lesley thought. All kinds of offers. 'Bambi, they're waiting for us.'

'I'm almost ready. I just wanted to tell you that I feel real comfortable with you, Miss Allen. I really like you.'

'We probably have a lot in common,' Lesley said. It was humbling to realise that ten years ago she must have resembled this woman closely. She couldn't imagine that Cade's taste in companions would have changed much—so she must have been the one who had done the changing.

When they rejoined the two men Bambi's face lit up as she heard the music coming from the dimly lit dance floor. 'Let's go dance, Cade,' she demanded, tapping her foot.

But Cade shook his head, and Bambi looked disappointed as she slouched down in her chair, her bright lips pouting. Jay sat down next to her and asked a low-voiced question. It seemed to entertain her, for she sat up and answered brightly.

Cade didn't seem to notice Bambi's mood change; he pulled out the chair next to Lesley's.

'Do you know, Miss Allen,' he told her, looking out over the crowded dance floor, 'I am constantly amazed by young women like you.'

Jay was smiling. 'Lesley is amazing. There's nothing she can't do. It would take three people to replace her at the magazine.'

'Today's Woman,' Cade mused.

Lesley wondered if she was imagining the note of sarcasm in his voice. Then he continued, and she knew that she hadn't been mistaken.

'She lives her career, controls everyone around her, hungers for even more power, from the bedroom to the boardroom. You've been at the magazine for several years. What's left, Miss Allen? Where do you go from here?'

'Who said I was going anywhere?' she parried.

He smiled. 'Don't play games. You're too ambitious to stop where you are. Tell me about your dreams.'

What harm could there be in telling him? It wouldn't hurt for him to know that she had other possibilities, that she didn't have to work for the *Woman*. She sipped her Perrier and said composedly, 'I want to start a new magazine. *Today's Woman* is fine, but it's aimed at the woman with a job and a family.'

He raised an eyebrow. 'What other kind is there, these days?'

'There's an entire market that we're missing. The career woman. Your description wasn't very flattering, Mr Randall, but there are a lot of those women out there—professional women, who aren't interested in pre-schools and quiltmaking, and yet aren't radically into women's rights, either. Women who still like to have doors held for them, but who are quite willing to hold them for other people too. The kind of woman that you don't believe exists, Mr Randall.'

'Oh, I believe she exists. There are thousands of them, the women who are competing with men everywhere. Even in bed—though an amazing number of them are frigid.'

Lesley raised her glass to her lips, staring at him over the rim. 'You sound angry. Have you been frozen by a few of them, Mr Randall?' she asked sweetly. 'Women are not just for housekeeping and childbearing, you know.'

'I never said they were.'

Lesley let her gaze light on Bambi, and said thoughtfully, 'No, perhaps you didn't. It must be hard for you to believe that certain women would put a career ahead of a man—even a man like you, Mr Randall.' Her voice was sweet. 'Some of them would say—especially a man like you.'

'Now, Angel—now, really, Lesley.' Jay was stumbling over himself to keep the discussion from escalating into a disastrous argument.

Cade's smile was dangerous. 'My intuition says you're one of those women, Miss Allen.'

'I put my career ahead of some men—certainly, Mr Randall.' Her voice was cool.

Jay scrambled for another topic of conversation. 'Cade, are you going to let Lesley interview you for the magazine? Whether we reach an agreement on the sale or not, the readers would love it.'

Cade smiled. 'Oh, I'd be delighted. I'd like to watch the lady work.' His voice was silky. 'As a matter of fact, perhaps you'd like to see the rest of the magazines the Randall Group publishes.'

'I'm familiar with the list,' Lesley said.

Jay laughed. 'At least one of them is not to her liking, Cade. She detests *Monsieur*—but she also admits that she doesn't read it regularly.'

'You disappoint me, Miss Allen. I should have thought, with your liberal attitudes ... I'll start a subscription for you right away.'

'No, thank you.'

'Oh, I insist. My gift, of course. Shall we consider the discussion at an end and go dance, Miss Allen?'

There was no tactful way to say no; Lesley let him lead her on to the dance floor.

Me and my big mouth, she thought crossly. She should have known better than to cross swords with Cade Randall. But that monumental ego of his had been too big a temptation.

Well, she'd show him that she could dance with him and stay totally unmoved. She tried to maintain a little distance as he put his arms around her.

He angled a look down at her, his eyes gleaming. 'Play fair, Miss Allen,' he said, and she reluctantly relaxed.

His arms tightened, and her breath caught at the sensation that swept through her. The heat of his body seemed to burn through the satin and scorch her delicate skin. She felt the muscles in his shoulders ripple under her hand.

It's like making love in slow motion, she thought, her brain drugged by his nearness. He consumes all the oxygen in the room; no wonder it's so hard to breathe.

And then she thought, don't be ridiculous, Lesley. He's no big deal—just an overwhelmingly conceited man who learned how to make a pass when he was still in his cradle.

His breath stirred her hair as he said, 'Career women—how can you work at such a pace all day, dance all night, and still take care of yourself and raise your child . . .'

She missed a step and her foot came down squarely on top of his. 'I'm sorry,' she said breathlessly, and plunged on without thought, anxious to deny his assumption. 'You misunderstood, Mr Randall. I don't have a child. I've never been married.' She tipped her head back to look at him with challenge in her eyes. Despite her high heels, it seemed like a long way up to his face.

'One doesn't have to be married, Miss Allen.'

'That goes without saying. Nevertheless, I don't have a child.'

'How very interesting,' he purred. 'But that means that what you told me a long time ago wasn't true. You should consider the consequences before you tell lies, Lesley.' There was steel under the calm words, and a sarcastic twist to the way he said her name.

She was silent a long time, her body moving mindlessly in his grip. How long was this dance going to last, she wondered. He pulled her even closer on the crowded floor, and she seemed to melt into him. It angered her, that her body responded to him unconsciously, and she could have kicked herself for getting involved in that crazy discussion. If she had stayed silent instead of drawing his attention to her . . . Stop the wishful thinking, Lesley, she told herself firmly. It's too late now to take back those rash words.

Finally her voice came back. 'So you do remember me.'

'Don't flatter yourself. I remember the twenty thousand dollars it cost me to get rid of you. You were a very expensive virgin, Lesley.'

Of course. How silly of her to have forgotten that money had been involved. 'You're the one who set the price, Mr Randall.'

'Don't you think our ·... prior acquaintance ... allows you to call me Cade?' His hands were sliding casually over the back of her gown and the bare skin above it.

Lesley gritted her teeth; there was no way to stop him, and she resolved that she would never again set foot on a dance floor with Cade Randall.

Then she almost laughed at herself. He was exacting his revenge, and when this dance was done, it would be all over. She'd be finished at the magazine, of course, if he bought it. She'd have to hurry if she was going to resign rather than be fired. At the moment, it didn't seem to matter.

He said thoughtfully, 'You wrote to me that you were expecting my baby. And the evidence you sent along was fairly compelling. Now here you are—with no nine-year-old at your side. Tell me, Lesley—did you abort my child? Or did you lie when you said you were pregnant?'

Her throat was tight. 'It can't have been the first time it happened,' she parried. 'Good old Mr—what was his name? Thornton, that was it—your faithful Mr Thornton must have investigated a hundred girls who said you'd made them pregnant.'

'He probably has.' Cade didn't sound interested. 'I'm sure you won't believe me when I say that I'd never slept with most of them.'

'You're right. I don't believe you.'

'But you were the only one who ever convinced him. You're quite an unusual lady, Lesley Allen. The only one who ever made Mr Thornton come back to me in a sweat and say that I'd better pay or there would be a court judgment against me and a child running around Illinois carrying my name.'

'What happened to the rest of them?'

'The ones who were foolish enough to sue were thrown out of court.' He didn't seem to care. 'In fact, Mr Thornton was amazed when you took the first offer we made. He wanted me to start the bidding much higher. If you'd held out, my dear, you could have had five times what you got.'

Lesley shrugged. 'It was my inexperience, I suppose. I thought I'd better take what was offered.'

'Which was it, Lesley? Was there ever a child? I'll get the truth out of you eventually, you know. Delay, and you may not like my methods.'

'I lied.' The words seemed to catch in her throat.

His hold tightened for just an instant. Raw fear touched her spine; she was grateful that his hands hadn't been on her throat just then.

'Be glad that you didn't commit murder, Lesley.'

'Abortion?' Her voice was steady, but it took effort. 'Your readers would never recognise you now, Mr Randall.'

'The magazine is a business. It has its views; I have mine.' He looked out across the dancers, and his voice was hard. 'I'm glad you lied, Lesley. No child deserves to have a mother like you. I would have wanted better for my son or daughter.'

Her throat was tight. For an instant she longed to slap that handsome face, to scream that he was self-righteous and—and dead wrong. But she swallowed the accusation. 'In that case, perhaps you should be more selective about the women you sleep with,' she murmured.

He laughed. It wasn't a pleasant sound. 'That just leaves us with the matter of this loan to discuss. Twenty thousand dollars at ten percent interest—you'll notice that I'm being liberal with the rate—compounded quarterly . . . Well, the accountants will have to figure it all out, but it looks to me as if you owe me just about fifty thousand dollars.' He looked down at her with one eyebrow raised. 'Would you care to discuss repayment terms? I'm sure you could think of some interesting ones.'

'I'll give you a cheque.' Anything to get rid of him, she thought. She had part of the money; she had even tried to put back what she had spent on her education. Of course, she had spent three thousand dollars on . . . She forced the thought to the back of her mind.

The dance ended, and they started towards the table, picking their way through the crowd. She knew that he was looking at her through narrowed eyes, and sensed that he was disappointed. Of course he would be, she realised. He wouldn't expect that she would have that much cash. A girl who conned a wealthy man out of twenty thousand dollars didn't usually put it in a savings account.

Well, he didn't need to know that she didn't have it all. If she had to mortgage everything she owned, she would; surely she could lay her hands on that much cash.

'Just a small cheque on Jay's account?' he jibed.

'From my own funds!' she snapped. 'This whole thing has nothing to do with Jay.'

'I'm not certain Jay would agree. But I'll stop by the magazine tomorrow to see if you can come up with the money.'

'It will be there.'

'I'm not holding my breath,' he said, and pulled out her chair with elaborate care.

*   *   *

It was the nearest they had ever come to having an argument. Jay was fuming by the time he parked the Mercedes in the ramp behind the Metro Tower. 'What in the hell is the matter with you, Lesley?' His voice was coldly furious, but it was still soft.

Lesley noted with calm interest that he wasn't using her pet name any more. 'Are you coming up to the condo, Jay?'

'You sounded like some kind of sex maniac! If my mother had heard you . . .'

'I doubt your mother and Cade Randall move in the same circles, Jay.'

'To say nothing of jeopardising the sale with every word you said! This is not a game we're playing here, Lesley. It's a matter of fifteen million dollars!'

'Is that how much you're asking?' She considered the figure, and shook her head. 'I doubt he'll pay that much.'

'I didn't expect he would, but now he may call the whole thing off, Lesley, how could you do this to me? How could you endanger our future?'

'Cade Randall has been around far too long to let anything interfere with business. If he wants the magazine, he'll buy it no matter what I say to him. And if he doesn't want it, he won't pay fifteen dollars for it—much less fifteen million. He won't keep me around, of course, but then I wasn't planning to stay anyway.' She stopped at the door of her apartment. 'And as for me coming across like a sex maniac . . . Isn't that how you phrased it?'

'That's what it sounded like to me. You were carrying on a conversation about his consuming interest in sex—my God, Lesley!'

'Cade Randall has never looked at a woman in any terms other than sexual. I could have been sitting there in a dirty potato sack, and he'd still have been undressing me in his mind.' And with the memory the man had, no doubt he'd been fairly accurate too, the little voice in the back of her brain reminded.

'You sound as if you know him.'

She swallowed hard. 'He doesn't trouble to keep his views secret, Jay.'

'Well, you didn't have to goad him about it. All that garbage about women wanting the freedom of the bedroom . . .'

'Jay——' She turned to face him and laid a slender hand on the velvet lapel of his jacket. 'I really believe all that.'

He turned white. 'But Angel, you've never . . .'

'No, I've never played hopscotch from bed to bed. It was never right for me. But I do believe in sexual freedom as a principle. Why should the double standard still operate? If a man can have a dozen affairs before he marries, why should he expect his bride to be a virgin?'

He sighed. 'I don't want to argue about it, Lesley. I just want to know why in the hell you thought it was up to you to convert Cade Randall to your way of thinking.'

She didn't have an answer to that. He wouldn't understand that seeing a ghost from her past had suddenly stripped all sense from her head. 'I'll see you tomorrow, all right?'

She ducked her head to avoid his kiss and put her key in the lock.

'Angel?'

'I'm sorry, Jay.' She closed the door softly behind her and leaned against it, weariness dragging at her bones. Then she went straight to the little office tucked away under the balcony bedroom and yanked the cover off the typewriter. It was the best therapy she knew.

She looked at the first page of her manuscript, and then she dropped the sheaf of paper in the wastebasket with an air of finality.

The sun found her there in the morning when it peeked over Lake Michigan. She was sound asleep in the white wicker chair, the red satin dress crumpled, her head pillowed on a stack of new manuscript pages atop the typewriter.

CHAPTER THREE

HER desk was, not surprisingly, just as deep in work to be done as it had been when she left the previous afternoon, and Lesley sighed when she saw it. It hadn't been too wise to stay up all night, she chided herself, and then concluded that she probably couldn't have slept anyway.

She set her briefcase on a chair, tucked a loose strand of hair back into the knot at the nape of her neck, and smoothed the draped neckline of the pure-white dress. The dress was absolutely plain, and she had left it innocent of accessories today, except for the antique gold setting of the diamond on her left hand.

Shelah tapped on the door and came in, carrying a mug of coffee. She wordlessly handed it across the desk to Lesley, who drank half of it at a gulp.

'The art director wants to see you. He's got a new design idea for the winter fashion layout.'

Lesley groaned. 'I thought I told him exactly what I wanted.'

'You have, once a week for the last month. He still isn't listening, and it should have been done yesterday.' She reached across the desk for Lesley's appointment calendar. 'Shall I call a special staff meeting this morning? Next Monday is deadline, and since you've been gone all week . . .'

'Please. Eleven o'clock.'

'It will have to be a short one if we start so late,' Shelah warned. 'Half the staff always has a lunch date.'

Lesley smiled, the dimple peeking out for the first time all morning. 'I know. That's the general idea; it cuts the nonsense to a minimum.' She shifted a stack of correspondence to the corner of her desk. 'Tell the art director I'll see him for fifteen minutes before the meeting. Did you talk to our friendly advice columnist?'

'No. She left town right after she called yesterday. I used to think I'd like to have your job,' Shelah mused, 'but fortunately I've come to my senses.'

Lesley scanned another letter and added it to the stack. 'Well, if you don't want to be editor, you'd better scream and run.'

Shelah removed Lesley's briefcase from a chair and sat down, crossing her legs. 'All right,' she demanded. 'I'm sitting here till you explain that.'

Lesley shrugged. 'I just mean that I can't work for the man who's thinking about buying it. So the instant Jay signs his name on the bill of sale, I sign my letter of resignation. And you're next in line—at least temporarily.' Then she added thoughtfully, 'Unless Mr Randall brings in someone from another magazine.'

'Which he might, of course.' Shelah looked thoughtful.

'You don't sound surprised.'

'I'm not. Rumours have been going around about the Randall Group being interested.'

'I certainly hadn't heard them.'

'But then you were off talking to Derek Stone. It's even been said that Cade Randall called Jay first, and not the other way around.'

Lesley considered that, and dismissed it. Cade might pick up *Today's Woman* if it fell in his path, but she didn't think he wanted it badly enough to make the first approach.

'It might be fun to work for Cade Randall,' Shelah mused. 'His magazines share a lot of resources.'

Lesley looked up from the article she was skim-reading. 'You're just thinking about all those young, intense reporters at the news magazine.'

'Absolutely not,' Shelah denied. Then she grinned. 'I'm thinking about all of the men he has working for him, everywhere. Did Jay give you the whole story?'

'We had dinner with Mr Randall last night.' Lesley spread copy and photographs out on the drawing board and tried to look absorbed.

Shelah was properly impressed. 'Tell me, is he really as handsome as his pictures?'

'I didn't notice.'

'Lesley, you're hopeless. How could you ignore those broad shoulders, and the big brown bedroom eyes, and that hair that makes any sane woman want to run her fingers through it?'

'It was very easy.' It was only a white lie, she told herself. She handed the article to Shelah. 'That piece needs eight more lines taken out of it.'

Shelah groaned. 'I edited it as tightly as I could already. I was certain it would fit.'

'Sorry. I'm not carrying it over to another page for just eight lines.'

Shelah flipped through the copy. 'Whatever you say, boss. Did he make a pass at you last night? Or didn't you notice that either?'

'He made several.' Lesley opened another folder and laid the sketches it contained out on the board.

'Oh, now I know why you don't want to work for him. His unsavoury reputation.'

'That's a polite way to put it.'

Shelah shrugged. 'Well, not every man can be a Jay Nichols, thank God. I've always wanted to know, Lesley—what do you see in Jay, anyway?'

'He's gentle and caring and a warm human being.' Her blue pencil flashed over the captions, checking for clarity and double meanings.

'He's a marshmallow,' Shelah said cruelly. 'He probably smiled vaguely all the time Cade Randall was flirting with you. Either he was too dumb to know what was going on or too chicken to do anything about it. Lesley, when are you going to discover men?'

'I have no need of a cave man in my life, if that's the kind you're talking about.'

'A man doesn't have to be primitive to want to protect his woman. I bet it's been years since Cade Randall had to drag a woman anywhere, but he wouldn't sit by quietly and watch someone else make a pass at her.'

'I'm shocked, Shelah. I've thought all along that you were liberated, and now I find out it was just a front.'

'It doesn't necessarily imply ownership if a man is protective. And for that matter, Jay certainly feels as if you belong to him. He acts as if that ring you wear is a ball and chain.'

'So perhaps that's why he doesn't feel it necessary to challenge Cade Randall to a duel,' Lesley said gently.

Shelah sighed. 'That reputation of his is all a publicity stunt, anyway. Especially all those models he's seen with. Every one he shows up with at a nightclub sells another thousand copies of *Monsieur*.'

Lesley looked up from the drawing board, a glint in her eyes. 'Why don't you do the maths on that problem, Shelah? Compare how much profit he makes on a thousand copies against how much the date costs him.'

'It's a business expense.'

Lesley laughed. 'A very interesting business our Mr Randall runs.'

'He's not just seen with models, either. The last publicity pix I saw Marissa Benton was on his arm.'

'Too bad it wasn't in person. You could have asked her why she divorced our favourite Derek.' Lesley put the layout back in the portfolio and added another item to her list of things to be done.

'Maybe I will call her,' Shelah picked up the list. 'Lesley, this list is ridiculous.' She reached for another slip of paper, and transferred half of the items to it, crossing them off the original list. She waved the new list at Lesley. 'I'd better get busy,' she said. 'I'll see you at the staff meeting.'

Lesley looked at her own list again and had to smile. Shelah had assumed several of the chores that she knew Lesley hated, but she had also volunteered to call the young paediatrician about the new column. Well, Shelah wanted him, and she usually got her way.

Lesley felt a little better about the future of the magazine. Shelah was a darn good editor. The rest of her staff would be like lambs thrown to the slaughter if they came up against Cade Randall, but Shelah could hold her own as an editor and as a woman. If he would just give her that chance ...

She was already assuming that Cade would buy the magazine, Lesley realised. Don't give up, she told herself. A lot of things could happen yet.

The top-level staff was waiting for her in the conference room at eleven. Lesley commented on their promptness, and took her own chair at the head of the table. They were always working on at least three issues at once, and keeping everything co-ordinated was an exhausting challenge. Perhaps Shelah was right, she thought; maybe she was trying to do too much.

There were two surprises waiting for her when she came back to her office after the staff meeting. The first was pleasant—a dozen roses the colour of rich cream, their petals heavy with fragrance, were on the corner of her secretary's desk, still partially wrapped in green tissue paper, the tiny card addressed to Angel peeking out from the glossy dark foliage.

The second, less pleasant, surprise was Cade Randall, lounging in a comfortable chair beside Jana's desk.

She stopped in the doorway when she saw him there, then walked straight across to the flowers to take a deep breath of their heady fragrance.

'Jay has expensive taste in roses, I'll grant him that. I came for a tour of the office,' he explained without waiting for her question. 'Then I'll take you to lunch. Jana assures me you don't have a date.' His eyes roved over her, missing nothing from high-heeled sandals to the smooth knot of her hair.

And next week Jana might not have a job, either, Lesley told herself. 'You didn't bring Bambi,' she said, raising an eyebrow.

'Bambi is not a businesswoman.'

'You could engrave that on her tombstone,' Lesley said tartly. 'Come on in.'

'Don't forget your flowers, Lesley,' her secretary reminded.

Cade reached for the vase. 'Since you have your hands full,' he said, following her into the inner office. She'd never seen a man who didn't look ridiculous with his arms full of flowers, but Cade managed it. He set the roses on her desk with a flourish and gestured toward the slatted blinds on the glass wall. 'Shall I close these so we can have a private chat?'

'I've never found it necessary. The room is soundproof.' Lesley put the stack of folders on the corner of her desk. She liked being able to look out over the busy floor and see what her staff was doing.

He closed the blinds anyway. Lesley sighed and asked, 'Have you proved your point?' She sat down in the swivel chair behind her desk and gave him the same degree of wary attention that she would have awarded a troublesome advertising account.

'You run a very casual office,' he observed.

'Do you mean the mess on my desk? It's stacked so high because I've been gone most of the week.'

'I mean the fact that your secretary uses your first name. Does everyone call you Lesley?'

She looked him over carefully. Last night he'd been wearing dark brown evening clothes. Today it was a coffee-coloured three-piece suit, probably a cashmere blend, she decided, with a yellow silk shirt. A discreet diamond tiepin nestled in his striped tie. He could have stepped from the pages of one of his own magazines.

'Not everyone is invited to use my first name, Mr Randall.'

He grinned, and crinkly lines appeared at the corners of his dark eyes. It made him look suddenly very much like the Cade she had met ten years ago, and Lesley had to take a firm grip on herself. 'If that's a roundabout way to tell me that I'm not one of the select few, I plan to ignore it, my dear.'

She shrugged. 'I find we get more work done in an informal atmosphere. Are you objecting?'

'Not necessarily. It was only a comment, not an

accusation.' He glanced at the flowers. 'Aren't you going to look at the card?'

'I didn't want to be rude. At any rate, since the envelope says they're for Angel, I thought—as you did—that the source was obvious.' She reached for the tiny card.

'Are they Jay's way of saying thank you for last night?' he speculated. 'A whole dozen roses—you must have had a good time after you left the restaurant.'

The card just said, 'I'm sorry, darling.' She tucked it back into the flowers and ignored his question.

'Does he always call you Angel?'

Lesley smiled unwillingly as she remembered how angry Jay had been last night. 'Almost always.'

'Don't you ever get tired of it? And don't you ever wonder if he uses a pet name so he won't accidentally call you Joyce?'

'It had never occurred to me.'

He raised an eyebrow. 'Perhaps I just have a nasty mind, but . . .'

'No truer words were ever spoken.'

He looked injured. 'Please, Lesley. Don't be snide. Does he call you Angel in bed, too?'

She refused to be drawn.

'To put it delicately, don't you ever wonder if Joyce was also his angel?'

'She wasn't.'

'White roses,' he mused. 'Quite suitable for an angel. Or for a virgin. But, sadly, not appropriate for you. I'd have sent red ones. They're much more your style, for the fire that's buried deep inside you.' There was a thoughtful pause. 'I wonder if Jay has ever seen that fire?'

'Does it amuse you to speculate about me?'

He didn't answer. 'Or perhaps you aren't even sleeping with Jay. Is he waiting till you're married because he thinks you're a virgin?'

She stood up. 'Do you want a tour, or did you just come in to harass me?'

He looked surprised. 'Of course I want a tour. I just signed an option on the magazine this morning—I would like to see what I'm bidding on.'

'Does that make it official? You're going to buy the *Woman*?'

'I'm not certain yet. The option just says that Jay can't sell it to anyone else for the next sixty days. I'll know by then if I want it or not.' He stayed in his chair. 'I also came in for my money—if you remember?'

'Oh.' She sat down again, feeling a little foolish.

'Of course, we could talk about options, if you don't have the fifty-one thousand, eight hundred, and . . .' he patted his waistcoat pockets. 'I have the exact amount here somewhere. That's compounded annually, of course—my accountant said it really wasn't fair to make it quarterly.'

'Are you going to tell Jay?'

'Will I have to?' he countered.

Lesley reached for her handbag. 'I hope my personal cheque is good enough.'

'Are you certain you don't want to hear about the options?' He came around the desk and leaned over her chair.

'I'm positive.' Her fountain pen wavered a bit, and the date came out a little wobbly. She took a deep breath and wrote his name.

'I thought about it all night, and I came up with some very original payment plans.'

'I'd prefer to pay cash. How much did you say it was?' It would drain her reserves, overdraw her bank account, and force her to put a second mortgage on the condo. But she supposed that she was fortunate to be able to get the money. His idea of repayment made her shiver.

'Fifty thousand even will be fine. I'll forgive the other two-thousand-odd.'

She frowned. A note of generosity didn't sound like him.

'I only deal in even numbers,' he added easily.

She wasn't about to argue. It would be two thousand less to explain to her banker. She ripped the cheque out and handed it to him.

'I love the green ink,' he said. 'It matches your eyes.' He tipped up her chin. 'I'll be darned. They've changed again. What colour are they, anyway?'

'None of your business.'

'Hazel, perhaps? And they must change shades depending on what you wear. The white dress today makes them look brown. Your eyes are fascinating, Lesley. They probably change with your mood, too. I'll bet that when you're in bed, they're smoky grey. Almost black.'

'You should remember,' she said icily.

'Sorry I didn't notice. Give me another chance? I'll pay special attention this time.'

'Never. The tour leaves now, if you're coming.'

He blew on the ink and tucked the slip of paper into the watch pocket of his waistcoat. 'As a matter of fact, I am glad you had the money. Explaining the payment plans to Jay might have been a little sticky. Let's have lunch before the tour.'

'I don't want to have lunch with you.'

He looked very sad. 'I'd hate to have to tell Jay that you aren't co-operating,' he said softly.

'I just work for the magazine. I'm not involved in the sale.' She didn't look at him.

'A couple of weeks ago he asked for all possible co-operation from the staff.'

Lesley looked up from the file folder she had opened. Her eyes widened in shock. 'How did you know that? It was a private memo.'

'I read a lot of memos.'

'Is someone on my staff providing you with inside information?'

'If you'd like me to answer that question . . .' he checked his watch. 'I made a reservation, and we're going to be late as it is.'

Lesley sighed and gave in. She took her light grey

coat from the closet where she always left it and sneaked a look in the mirror at her make-up. It would do; she wasn't going to stand there in front of Cade and apply fresh lipstick.

He held the coat for her, then turned her to face him and settled the lapels with proprietary care, smoothing the fabric over her shoulders. 'I was right,' he said. 'Now your eyes are grey. But not passionate grey.'

'Yours are going to be black if you don't take your hands off me,' she warned.

He straightened the brilliant red scarf that lay under the coat collar, the single bright accent. Then he shook his head, and his eyes sparkled. 'Jay wouldn't do anything that might upset his sale.'

'Jay wouldn't have to. I would do it all by myself.'

'I'd like to see you try.' His hands slid over her shoulders and down her spine, drawing her close. Then he bent his head, and his mouth was suddenly warm and caressing against hers.

With a supreme effort of will, she stayed absolutely quiet in his arms. But he didn't seem disturbed by her lack of response. When he released her, he merely said, 'Poor Jay. What's happened to you in the last ten years? I don't remember you being an ice sculpture.'

'Perhaps I'm not cold when I'm with Jay.' She tipped up her head with a challenge in her eyes. Even with the high-heeled shoes she wore, he was a head taller.

He laughed. 'Jay Nichols couldn't warm up a bed if he had an electric blanket to help.' His fingertips slid gently down over her breast.

'I'm an engaged woman, Mr Randall.'

He picked up her left hand and inspected the diamond ring. 'Do you know, I never did believe in engagement rings,' he said, and pulled open the door.

Jana looked up with a smile. Lesley wondered, from the girl's expression, if Cade had lipstick all over him. It would not surprise her if she had failed to notice it.

'I'll be at——' Lesley looked up at Cade expectantly, waiting for him to supply the name of the restaurant.

'We will be out to lunch,' he told Jana, and tucked Lesley's hand into his arm. 'The *Woman* will not fall apart if you are out of touch for an hour and a half. You really must learn to delegate responsibility,' he told her in the elevator.

'I really must start getting some work done.'

'Lesley, you're spreading yourself too thin. You're administrator, editor, and writer. If I decide to buy the *Woman*, you aren't going to be all three anymore. You might start thinking about which job you want to keep.'

'Look, Mr Randall, if you're trying to convince me that I wouldn't be happy at the *Woman* anymore, you can save your breath. The moment Jay signs that contract, I will resign before you have a chance to fire me. All right?'

This time the surprise on his face looked real. 'Why would I fire you?'

Lesley laughed. 'Because of the cheque in your pocket, for one.'

He shook his head. 'I didn't get where I am by holding grudges. You owed me some money—you paid it. The decks are clear.'

'I don't believe you.'

He shrugged and pushed the revolving door. 'Whatever you say, Lesley. We're going to Cicero's— shall we walk or take a cab?'

'Italian?' She shook her head. 'Too many calories.'

'It looks as if you could use a few. What are you doing, anyway? Starving yourself so you can start modelling for your own covers, too?'

She gave in. 'All right, I'll have a salad. Let's walk.'

'You'll have something more substantial than that if I have to feed you myself.'

Lesley stopped in the middle of the pavement, hands deep in her pockets. 'You really are a tyrant, aren't you? I noticed you wouldn't even let Bambi order her own drink last night.'

He wrapped the long red scarf about her throat. 'Bambi always drinks Margueritas, and she can never remember the name of them. It's easier not to ask her what she wants.'

She promptly unwrapped the scarf and let the ends dangle to the hem of her coat. 'Well, I'm not Bambi, so don't start bossing me around, Mr Randall,' she said. 'I can take care of myself.'

He fell silent, and Lesley congratulated herself. Take that, Cade Randall, she thought.

But she promptly spoiled the effect two blocks later when she tripped over the threshhold at Cicero's. Cade caught her. His arm was like steel as he pulled her back on to her feet.

'Thanks.' Lesley had to grit her teeth to say it.

He raised a dark eyebrow. 'If you will insist on wearing six-inch heels, you might consider keeping a man around at all times.'

'They're not six-inch heels, and I don't need a man!'

His grin told her that once again she had reacted exactly as he'd expected. 'Is that why you're marrying Jay Nichols?' he asked sweetly.

Their table was secluded in a corner. They might almost have been the only patrons.

Cade looked around with a satisfied sigh. 'The best food in the city,' he said. 'I consider a trip here wasted if I don't eat at Cicero's.'

'How often do you come to Chicago, anyway?'

'Three or four times a year. I'm not travelling as much as I used to, and I've given up the lecture circuit entirely.'

Lesley became very absorbed in her menu. She hoped that the colour wasn't rising in her face. It had been one of those lectures that had brought him to southern Illinois ten years ago, when she had still been a high school student and he had been the heir, not the owner, of the Randall Group.

'Besides, I always bring my dates here.'

'This is not a date, it is a business lunch.' Lesley fought to keep her voice from rising.

He looked thoughtful. 'Perhaps you're right. Would you like some wine?'

'I don't drink at lunch.'

'You don't drink much of anything any more. You used to, if I remember correctly.'

'You remember too darn much. And, if you think about it, perhaps that will explain why I'm more careful these days.'

The waiter arrived, and Cade looked up. 'We would like the linguini with clams. Oh, yes—the lady has also requested separate checks.'

'You invited me to lunch,' Lesley reminded. 'In fact, you gave me very little choice.'

He shrugged. 'I only pay when it's a date.'

'All right. If I'm paying for my own food, I'll have a chef's salad,' Lesley snapped.

The waiter's head swivelled in confusion as his eyes darted back and forth between them. He finally said, trying to be firm, 'No separate checks, sir.'

Cade closed his menu. 'In that case, bring her the linguini and me the bill,' he instructed the waiter gently. 'And I'd like a cup of coffee.'

'It comes with the meal, sir,' the waiter said, relieved to have the problem solved.

Lesley handed over the menu and glared at Cade. 'So I end up with a plate of linguini I don't want.'

'I can recommend it. It's the best you'll find anywhere in the Midwest.'

'Paying for my lunch is the least you could do. You brought me here against my will, after all.'

'I also just forgave a two-thousand dollar debt. Perhaps you should take me out to lunch.'

'You said a minute ago that it was all over and forgotten.'

'I said I wasn't going to let it interfere with your job, which you are very good at. Of course, you could just interview me while we eat, and then the bill could go on your expense account,' he pointed out.

'I have no intention of interviewing you, Mr Randall.'

He raised an eyebrow again. 'My pride is injured. Don't you think your readers would be interested?'

'When we go back to the *Woman*, I'll introduce you to Shelah Evans. She's my assistant editor, and an excellent writer.' Shelah would love to interview Cade, and it would bring her to his attention and help to assure that she would get a chance at the editorship when Lesley resigned. My good deed for the day, Lesley told herself.

'You do the interview, or it doesn't get done.'

Lesley folded her hands under her chin. 'But Mr Randall,' she said gently, 'you told me to delegate responsibility.'

'Lesley, I'm about to delegate you over my knee. And would you cut out the "Mr Randall" stuff? I'm not a senior citizen, and after all, we are intimately acquainted.'

'I would hardly call it intimate,' she demurred. 'A single night a decade ago doesn't make us best friends.'

'I wasn't looking for a best friend,' he suggested silkily. 'Lesley, I'm amazed that I haven't heard from you again in the last ten years.'

She shrugged. 'Your Mr Thornton made it quite plain that the settlement I got would be the end of it.'

He ignored her. 'Of course, you haven't done badly on your own in the magazine business. But I am shocked that you didn't request a job to get you started.'

'Really, Cade,' she said, in the tone of a kindergarten teacher. 'Think about it. If I had, you'd have discovered long ago that I'd conned you.'

He sat back in his chair and stared at her till Lesley shifted uneasily. 'Why did you do it, Lesley? You're lucky, you know, that I didn't find out the truth then. I've mellowed over the years.'

If he had, it wasn't apparent, she thought.

'Was it your father's idea?' he pursued.

'Please. He was only my stepfather.' Her eyes shadowed as she remembered the events of that morning she had tried so hard to forget—the morning after the night of magic. Then she shrugged it painfully aside. 'Let's leave it, Cade. You have the money back. It no longer matters why I thought I had to have it.'

He shook his head, but he didn't pursue the subject. 'I wonder what happened to my coffee?' he mused.

Lesley breathed a sigh of relief and decided not to be alone with him again. She wondered if she could manage to pull it off.

CHAPTER FOUR

MUCH as she hated to admit it, the linguini was delicious, and Lesley was ravenously hungry. Cade watched her eat with satisfaction. 'How long has it been since you had a square meal?' he asked and pushed the loaf of crusty homebaked bread across the table to her.

She shook her head. 'No more, thank you,' she told him, and added, 'I'm an excellent cook, and I eat very well.'

The waiter cleared the table. 'Dessert, Ma'am? We have spumoni today,' he offered helpfully. Lesley shook her head, and the man looked hurt. 'Would you like your coffee now, sir?'

'Please,' Cade said firmly.

Lesley laughed. 'He said it came with the meal,' she pointed out. 'He didn't say when.'

Cade looked chagrined. He stirred the dark, aromatic brew and said, 'By whose definition do you eat well? No one—especially a woman—does when she's alone,' he disagreed.

'Who said I eat alone? Jay thinks I make the best wild rice in the world.'

'When do you find time to do all these homey things?'

She saw the denomination of the bill he put on the waiter's tiny tray, and was glad that he hadn't forced the issue of who paid for her lunch. It was going to be difficult enough to explain that badly overdrawn bank account without having to borrow from her friends. 'I cook on weekends.'

'You amaze me. You don't spend Saturday and Sunday at the *Woman*, too? Have you ever wondered if you're a workaholic, Lesley?'

'How do you think I got where I am? I didn't have a benefactor, so I had to do it on my own merits.'

51

He stirred the dregs of his coffee thoughtfully. 'I wonder if I can talk the waiter out of a second cup?' he mused. 'Now that you've got to the top, Lesley, why don't you slow down?'

She looked up in surprise. 'Isn't that unusual advice for you to be giving?'

'Not really. I've lost three of my best people in the last year. Two heart attacks and one nervous breakdown.'

'You probably drove them to it.'

'No. They never learned to play. No one is indispensable, Lesley.'

'Not even Cade Randall?' she mocked.

He shrugged. 'Not even me. I won't deny that I thought I was for a long time. But when enlightenment dawned, I started working forty hours a week instead of a hundred, and the Randall Group is doing as well as ever.'

'And your staff started having heart attacks.'

'They're not asked to work overtime.'

Lesley shook her head. 'It's a little different for me.'

'Why? Because you're trying to show a profit so Jay can sell the magazine? You're burning yourself out, and you aren't proving anything to me.' He was silent for a moment. 'Or are you earning a living for Jay? Beware, my dear, I don't know what kind of standards he insists on, but I ran into his ex-wife on my last trip to Paris and she could show us all a few ways to get rid of money.'

She said primly, 'Jay doesn't believe in wives supporting their husbands.'

Cade finished his coffee and gave up on the second cup. 'Does that translate into "Jay doesn't believe in working wives"? Are you going to retire if I buy the *Woman*?'

'I don't plan to ever retire. I'm only half-alive when I'm not working on a magazine.'

'Then you'd better stay with me, kid. There are a lot of magazines in Chicago, but I can't think of one that could give you the opportunities this one can.'

'If you buy it,' Lesley added.

'That's right.'

She thought it over. 'I'll take my chances with the others.'

He shrugged. 'Be my guest.'

Back at the magazine, Lesley got another shock. The drab little man who rose from the chair right outside her office door had a familiar face, and he carried a pen and a legal pad as if they were sword and shield.

'Lesley, you do remember my attorney, don't you?' Cade asked with a knowing smile.

'Mr Thornton,' she said quietly.

'Miss Allen.' It was a clipped formality. Obviously he had been prepared to see her, and just as obviously he found it less than pleasant.

Lesley led the way into her office and hung up her coat. It took an effort to stop shivering at the effect of seeing that man again. It was he who had cross-examined her, accused her, made her cry more than once with his accusations before he had gone back to Cade with his recommendation to pay her off.

'By the way, Thornton,' Cade said casually, tossing himself down in the chair behind Lesley's desk, 'you were wrong.'

'Sir?'

'Our lovely Lesley has admitted that she lied to you. The infallible Thornton fell for a beautiful face in distress. There was no pregnancy.'

The attorney looked injured. 'But, Mr Randall . . .'

'It was a scam, Thornton. Oh, don't look at me like that. I'm not going to have you shot at dawn because you made a mistake, man. The girl obviously belongs on stage.'

Lesley shut the closet door and tried not to look at the lawyer. But her eyes strayed towards him, and she coloured as she met his gaze. His eyes, magnified by the round lenses of his glasses, were puzzled.

'As a matter of fact,' Cade mused, 'it's some comfort to know that you're human after all, Thornton.' His long fingers reached restlessly for the card, still tucked into the roses. ' "I'm sorry, Angel"?' he quoted, eyebrows raised.

Lesley removed the card from his hand and dropped it into her briefcase. 'Something you wouldn't understand.'

He grinned, and Lesley felt herself start to blush. But he dropped the subject, asking instead, 'Are you ready for our tour, Lesley?'

Since he was occupying her chair, she had little choice. She led the way through the big communal office on her way to the test kitchens, muttering under her breath about the amount of work that needed to be done. If Cade Randall really cared about people being overworked, she thought, he'd have left her alone to do her job.

The head of the test kitchens was icing a heart-shaped gingerbread house with pink peppermint frosting, made with a special technique so it would hold up better under the strong photographic lights.

'That's the cover of our February issue,' Lesley pointed out. 'And if word gets out I'll know where it came from.'

'Probably someone's lucky guess,' Cade argued. 'After fifteen years in this business, I know how to protect a cover story, Lesley. And the best way I know is to say that a story is the cover when it really isn't.'

The cook giggled. Lesley glared at her. Cade's intuition was remarkable, she thought. The gingerbread house could have been the cover; how did he know it had been knocked out of the running? And again she wondered how he was getting the inside information.

Oh, quit it, Lesley, she told herself crossly. It was probably a lucky guess. And even if Cade knew everything that was going on inside *Today's Woman*, there was nothing that would discourage the purchase. She ran a clean ship.

'It's only October,' he added. 'Isn't it awfully early for a Valentine's Day issue?

'We always work three to six months ahead. This time of year, with a double-sized Christmas issue, we usually fall behind anyway.'

'How many on the kitchen staff?'

'Just one. She has a clean-up crew, of course.'

He raised an eyebrow. 'You do a lot of food features for a small staff. How do you manage your monthly recipe contest with one cook?'

'That's easy. Most of the recipes we publish are tested by the staff as a whole. We decided long ago that the main test a contest winner had to pass was to be simple enough for a non-professional cook to make it easily.'

'That makes sense.'

'So every month, right after deadline, everybody draws a recipe out of a hat, we all trample each other in the kitchen, and we have a party. The dish that gets the most votes wins the contest.'

He looked thoughtfully around the gleaming stainless steel kitchen. Mr Thornton took notes. Then Cade said, 'I just have one question. When's the next party?'

'Next Monday. The final copy has to be on the afternoon flight to make it to the printer on time. Once it's gone, we'll play all evening.'

'I can see that I'll have to teach you a new definition of play,' Cade mused. 'Is this party open to visitors?'

'Only if you join in the cooking.'

He thought it over. 'I make decent coffee,' he offered.

Lesley shook her head. 'You have to draw a recipe, just like everyone else.' She led the way into the testing lab, where a white-coated technician was chopping tray after tray of ice cubes in a long row of food processors. 'We test a different sort of small appliance every month. All the models get thirty days of heavy use—every brutal test that Carol can dream up. That's more abuse than they'd get in the average home in five years. Then we assess each model's performance. This report will be in December's issue, just in time for people who want to buy Christmas gifts.'

Cade shook his head. 'Aren't you trying to do too

much? It seems to me the resources are spread very thin.'

'Not according to the readers—it's one of our most popular features. I'd like to expand the department, of course. There are dozens of small appliances that we never have room for in the magazine.'

Mr Thornton made a note. Lesley, who had forgotten he was there, looked at him with brief disfavour.

Cade gave her a charming smile. 'He's my right hand,' he explained. 'And you should be flattered. He only writes down what he hears if I think it's a good idea.'

'Does he use sign language or mind-reading?' Lesley asked curtly.

Cade looked intrigued. 'I never asked. Thornton, do you read my mind?'

Mr Thornton looked up from his notepad. 'It's a matter of understanding your body language, sir.'

Lesley found herself thinking that Cade's body could speak volumes. He was so damned masculine that he didn't even have to look at a woman for her to know with every aching fibre of her being that he was there.

She was uncomfortably aware of his nearness as he walked along beside her, his hand on her arm or his sleeve brushing hers. The scent of his aftershave tickled her nose, and her fingers itched to push that stray strand of hair back off his forehead . . .

With a tremendous effort, she pulled her attention back to the tour and led them into the next lab.

The tour dragged on for more than an hour as Cade sampled and inspected and questioned. Shelah caught up with them in the needlework lab.

'We've got a problem, Lesley,' she said.

Lesley stepped outside the door, and Shelah held up an advertising slick. 'The ad department sold a full page, with copy to come later. Now the copy is here, and . . .'

Lesley sighed. 'That's the most insulting layout I've

seen in the last year.' She held it at arm's length. 'I have no problem with ads that show women admiring their sparkling clean kitchen floors. They're stupid ads, perhaps, but one does have to scrub the floor now and then. But any company that dresses its models up in kitten suits—with tails, too—to make the point doesn't belong in this magazine.'

'That's what I thought you'd say. I'll call the agency and tell them they'll have to substitute something.'

'I'll do it——' Then Lesley hesitated. In another month, Shelah would probably be dealing with the problem herself. She might as well start now. 'Go ahead. Let me know how it turns out, Shelah,' she said.

Cade was right about one thing, she thought as she rejoined the pair. Delegating responsibility did feel good sometimes.

'A magazine doesn't make money by turning down advertising,' Mr Thornton commented coldly.

Lesley fixed her gaze on the thinning hair at the top of his head. The man must be able to hear through walls, she thought. 'Pardon me. I assumed you were a lawyer, not an accountant,' she said gently.

'That's only common sense, Miss Allen,' he shrugged.

'Perhaps it is. You must also remember, however, that a magazine doesn't make money unless its subscribers like its philosophy. And my readers do not enjoy seeing women in kitten suits selling floor wax. They feel insulted.'

He made a note on the legal pad. 'Something will have to be done about that attitude,' he remarked.

'Mine or the subscribers'?' Lesley didn't wait for an answer. 'Until and unless Mr Randall purchases this magazine, I'm in charge of it. If you'd like, I'll suggest to my advertiser that his copy would fit right into *Monsieur*. Of course, I doubt he'd find the readership to his liking.'

Cade laughed. 'It's a draw, you two,' he declared. 'Don't upset the applecart, Thornton. The lady's making money.'

'I'm amazed that she doesn't take you to task for calling her a lady,' Mr Thornton murmured.

Lesley's temper flared. 'Are you suggesting that the term doesn't apply?'

His eyes flashed behind the thick lenses, but he backed down. 'No, Miss Allen. Of course not.'

'I don't object to the word when it's a term of respect, Mr Thornton. You see, unlike the radical women's groups, I enjoy being a woman and I like to be treated as a lady. I don't want to be a man—I just want an equal opportunity to do my job. And there are a lot of women out there just like me.'

'And those are the ones you want to start a new magazine for?' Cade had perched on the corner of a table to watch the argument.

'Exactly.' She regretted ever mentioning that dream. But at least Cade knew she meant her threat to leave *Today's Woman*.

He looked at his watch. 'We'll have to talk about that sometime, Lesley. Right now I have another appointment. Thanks for the tour.'

She fled to her own office, drained and exhausted. Shelah was sorting through the stacks of mail on Lesley's desk.

She looked up with a smile. 'Is he going to buy it?'

'It certainly looks that way.' The office looked tiny and closed in; Lesley opened the slatted blinds with relief. 'What are you doing?'

'I thought you could use some help. I'm having dinner with the paediatrician, by the way.'

'Well, don't stay out too late. Deadline is coming up fast and I need you here tomorrow morning.'

Shelah struck a horrified pose. 'Lesley, I have every intention of being in bed by ten.'

It didn't fool Lesley. 'I know. With the paediatrician.'

'Only if he's as cute as he sounds.' Shelah sat down, her elbow on the corner of the desk in a confiding pose. 'Lesley, his voice would melt a stone, it's so smooth and gentle. I have a mental picture already.'

'Just be certain you get a commitment from him to write a column.'

'First thing, boss.'

'How did the problem with the ad turn out?'

'The agency was horrified that someone considered their new layout to be sexist. Then they tried the old trick about how no one else objected.'

'And you said?'

'I told them I didn't care if everyone else in the world ran it, the *Woman* wouldn't. They're sending over another slick next week. It doesn't run till next month.'

'You did a good job while I was gone, Shelah.'

'Thanks.' Shelah picked up her pile of papers. 'I'll take care of these things, and then I'm off to get ready for dinner.'

'They can wait till tomorrow. They'd have to if I was doing them.'

'No problem. My date isn't till eight.'

'Fast work, if you intend to be in bed by ten.' Lesley reached for the microphone on the tiny tape recorder so she could dictate her answers to the letters remaining on her desk. 'Someday that dizzy-blonde routine of yours is going to get you in trouble, Shelah.'

Shelah leaned around the doorframe and smiled, perfect teeth gleaming. 'I know. But it's such fun, Lesley.'

Shelah might sleep with the pediatrician, Lesley knew, but if she did, it would be so discreet that no one would know who she was seeing. And it would never be allowed to interfere with the magazine's business. Lesley just hoped that Shelah's private joke never got back to the doctor.

She methodically ploughed through the stacks on her desk, answering all the correspondence, sorting the new fiction submissions and putting them away to be read next week, after deadline was safely past, checking her own staff's copy with a blue pencil that flashed through sentences and paragraphs. And she still had the Derek Stone article to finish and lay out.

She was doing far too much, she thought, looking up at the clock. The outer office was dark, the staff gone home to families and pets. She needed another assistant, one as efficient as Shelah. Her job should not keep her tied in the office so much.

She tossed the blue pencil down and walked across to the window. The days were shortening but the city's skyline was still distinct against the setting sun.

Sometimes, on days like this, she felt so lonely that she thought she would scream for someone to notice her, for someone to care that she existed.

There was Jay, of course. But Jay adored the surface Lesley, his cool, sophisticated Angel. The few times that she had let him see the turbulent soul beneath the surface, he had backed off, and she had quickly put on the smooth exterior again, frightened of what he might think of her if she let him see too much.

'I do love Jay,' she said, resting her forehead against the cool glass as she looked out across the city. 'I really do.' He was calm and gentle and soft-spoken, qualities that had been missing in her childhood. He was everything she wanted in a husband.

But she was still lonely. Sometimes she felt as if no one in the world knew the real Lesley. Perhaps no one ever would, she thought.

Her mother had cared about her, but Lesley's stepfather had been a bully who was jealous of his wife's child. Lesley's earliest memories were of lying in her bed, listening to them fight about her, hiding her tear-streaked face under her pillow so she didn't have to hear the sharp words.

The night he had blackened her mother's eye had also ended her struggle to gain her mother's attention. She understood then that life would be easier for both of them if Lesley made no trouble, asked no questions. She was ten years old, and after that she drifted into a shadowy world that was hers alone.

If no one cared about Lesley, she had decided, then Lesley would care for herself. She didn't exactly feel sorry for herself; she saw it as a matter of survival. So she lived in their house but apart from them, rushing towards the day when she was old enough to be independent. Mostly they left her alone.

Now and then her stepfather would lecture. Every boy she dated became the subject of a tirade. He would scream; Lesley would listen politely and then drift off to her room. Men were only after one thing from her, he told her again and again. He accused her of sleeping with every boy she went out with. Lesley didn't bother to defend herself. If it pleased him to think that, telling him the truth wouldn't change his opinion.

So she walked her own way. She dated when she felt like it, but she decided eventually that it wasn't worth the trouble it caused her. It was easier not to date than it was to listen to the lectures. And since she'd never met a male who was worth making a change in her plans for, she didn't find anything missing in her life. Lesley intended to make it on her own.

She stared out across the darkening city and sighed. 'You were absolutely ripe for trouble, Lesley,' she told herself. Anyone could have predicted what had happened when Cade Randall came into her life.

She was seventeen that winter. She'd speeded through high school and could have graduated at midyear, but her stepfather had refused his permission. He was no fool; he knew that once she was through school the annuity left by her father would disappear, and he had uses for that monthly cheque. So she quietly continued her part-time job and took some random classes at the college to kill time. It meant that she didn't have to spend much time at home, and when she was there she could always use homework as an excuse to stay in her room.

But one of the classes she had stumbled into was a survey of mass media, and the professor had worked for some of the big-name magazines. By midterm Lesley was hooked, the fascination of magazine publishing already weaving into her heart. She spent every spare moment in the professor's office, hoping to hear more stories.

And then the professor had arranged for Cade Randall to speak on campus.

The Randall Group was already one of the most prestigious corporations in the industry. *Monsieur* was in its infancy; it was Cade's creation, cover to cover. But there were magazines covering news and sports and cars and fashion and architecture—an information network that stretched across the nation.

It was an opportunity Lesley jumped at. If she could just meet Cade Randall, she thought, she could find out what it was really like. She had no dreams of anything more; she knew that a long, hard-fought college education lay between her and any possibility of the job she wanted. But she desperately wanted to meet the man, to hang on to his words, to share the air he breathed.

The professor gave in to her pleading and introduced her to Cade, and she listened to him from the front row, eyes glued to that strong, handsome face. And then— after the lecture . . .

She turned away from the window, disgust with herself flowing over her in a wave. How damned innocent could a girl be? she asked. Well, she hadn't stayed innocent long. Cade had taken care of that.

She sighed. What was past was gone. There was no sense in dwelling on it now. She sat down at her drawing board and looked out across the big office to the main entrance. A shadowy form stood in the hall, knocking on the plate-glass door.

The breath caught in her throat for an instant, before she realised that it was Jay. Then she hurried across the office to let him in.

'Why didn't you use your key?' she asked.

'Mainly because I don't have it with me. What were you doing in here? I thought you'd never hear me.'

'I was thinking.'

'It must have been heavy stuff.' He leaned over the drawing board, looking at the photographs that she had been arranging.

'Just about my childhood, and . . . things.' She should tell Jay, she thought. He had a right to know about her stepfather, and about Cade. Not his name, of course—Lesley would never tell anyone that she had been just another plaything for Cade Randall. But the episode had left scars, and the man who was to be her husband had a right to know what had caused them.

And just in case Cade decided to take that way of getting even, she wanted Jay to hear it first from her.

He looked interested. 'You've never mentioned your childhood before, Angel.'

'It wasn't a happy one. I don't like to think about it.' She took a deep breath. Now was as good a time as any, she supposed. 'Jay . . .'

'Perhaps you can tell me about it sometime. How late are you going to work? It's after eight now.'

She looked at him for a long moment. 'I think I'll quit. I didn't get much sleep last night.' She looked around the office and decided to let everything lie. She'd be back early in the morning anyway.

Jay reached for her key and locked the plate-glass door behind them. 'I had breakfast with Cade at his hotel this morning,' he said as they rode the elevator up ten floors.

'I wondered where he was staying.'

'Where do you expect? In a suite at the best hotel in town. He really knows how to travel. I think he's going to buy the magazine, Angel.' He followed her into the condo. 'We signed an option this morning, and it cost him a fair amount for me to say that I wouldn't talk to other possible buyers for sixty days. He's serious, or he wouldn't have invested that sort of money.'

Lesley led the way to the kitchen. 'Let's keep it, Jay,' she said suddenly. 'Please don't sell it.'

'You just never quit, do you, Angel?' He sat down on a high stool at the breakfast bar and folded his arms on the counter. 'It sounds as if that magazine is the most important thing in your life.'

'I love it, Jay.'

'And you'll still have it. Cade thinks you're a marvellous editor—he's quite willing to keep you on, thought I'm not sure it's such a good idea.'

'Why are you concerned?' Lesley investigated the inside of the refrigerator and took out eggs and cheese. She didn't really want to cook a meal, she just wanted something quick and easy.

'Because you spend too much time there. Cade's going to bring in more staff, if he buys it. That will help, but I'm still not sure I want to have you absorbed in the magazine.'

'Why don't you keep it and hire a bigger staff?'

He stared at her. 'Didn't you hear me, Angel? I'm not worried about you being around Cade, for heaven's sake—he won't be here, and anyway, his taste hardly runs to your sort of woman.'

'Gee, thanks.' Lesley cracked an egg on the edge of the countertop with far more force than was necessary.

'It was meant to be a compliment. You're much more intelligent than Cade's usual companions.'

She added another egg and whipped the mixture with a wire whisk.

'And you know the financial situation I'm in. Joyce cleaned out every other asset I had when she left, and my mother is in no humour to bail me out.'

'Have you asked her?'

'Yes, I've asked. She told me that my father was afraid I'd throw everything away on fast women—sorry, Angel . . .'

'I've been called worse.' She poured the mixture into an omelette pan.

'And that's why he left everything else in her control when he died. The *Woman* is the only thing I have left, Angel.'

'Have you tried to borrow the money?'

'If you want to see an angry old lady, watch my mother the day she finds out I'm borrowing against my inheritance. She plans to live another hundred years, you know.'

And to keep you tied to her apron strings the whole time, Lesley thought. 'Perhaps we should learn to live within our means, Jay.' That was more ironic than he would never know, she thought. After all, she was the one who had overdrawn her account today with that fifty-thousand dollar cheque. And forgotten to call the bank about it, she remembered abruptly. If Cade tried to cash that cheque before she talked to her banker, there would be a warrant out for her arrest.

Jay's face brightened suddenly. 'But there's good news, too. She's going to come to our wedding after all. In fact, she said she'd even have a small reception at the house.'

'Whoopee.' Lesley slid the omelette on to a plate and added a sprig of parsley. Cheese oozed out of the centre.

'Angel, it's a big concession for her to make. She was raised to think a marriage was insoluble.' He reached for a napkin. 'That looks delicious. Aren't you eating anything?'

Lesley wordlessly pushed the plate across the counter. Her appetite was gone.

He was halfway through the omelette when he spoke again. 'You are going to wear a formal gown and veil, aren't you?'

'I hadn't thought about it. Why?'

'Don't you think we should do it right, as long as we are getting married?'

Lesley was brewing a cup of tea. She looked up to ask dryly, 'Is it any more legal if I wear white?'

'I think Mother's right, Angel.'

'I suspected it was her idea.'

'She says a private ceremony with a judge will make it look as if we're hiding something. And after all, you're entitled to a big white wedding. It's your first marriage, after all, and you'll want to make a splash.'

'I do not want a big wedding. I want a simple civil ceremony with two witnesses, an orchid corsage and a wedding ring. All right?'

'But, Angel . . .'

'Whose wedding is this? Ours or your mother's?'

He emptied the plate. She rinsed it and put it in the dishwasher.

'I'll have to get home,' he said reluctantly. 'She'll be wondering where I am. We'll talk about the wedding later, all right? There's plenty of time.'

She walked him to the door and turned her cheek up for his kiss. But her heart wasn't in it tonight.

His hands tightened on her shoulders for a brief moment. 'Just be charming to Cade Randall, Angel. That's all I ask right now.' There was a pleading note in his voice.

Lesley nodded wearily. After all, she asked herself, just what else could she do?

CHAPTER FIVE

'WHAT did you say, Lesley? You want to borrow how much money?' The voice of her banker rose in shock.

Lesley held the phone away from her ear for a moment and looked around to be certain that no one was within hearing distance. Then she propped the phone between shoulder and ear and repeated patiently, 'I'm not taking a flyer in the stock market, Josh. I have to put my hands on twenty thousand dollars today. I thought a second mortgage on my condo would probably be the best. It's worth ten times that.'

He groaned. 'Lesley, you don't want much besides the moon, do you? How do you think this bank arranges mortgages, anyway? I can't just snap my fingers and give you the money.'

'When can I have it?'

'Half of the people who would have to approve have already left for a long weekend. I'll talk to them on Monday, and you might have the money Tuesday. That's assuming that they approve the loan,' he warned. 'They might, since the condo is worth so much more than when you bought it—but usually they don't touch second mortgages at all.'

'Tuesday?' Lesley's voice was small and defeated.

'What's the matter, Les? If it isn't the stock market, what is it that can't wait till Tuesday? Tell the blackmailer you can't pay him till next week.' He laughed heartily at his own joke.

That was just exactly what she'd have to do, Lesley was thinking. And if Cade wasn't in a mood to wait for it . . . She'd better find an opportunity to tell Jay very, very soon.

'Why don't you cash your money-market certificates?' the banker asked. 'It'll cost you a penalty, but you can have the money today.'

'I already have,' Lesley admitted wearily.

There was an instant of silence. Then he said, with genuine alarm, 'Just what in the hell is going on, Lesley? There must have been thirty thousand dollars in that money-market fund.'

'There was, Josh.' No point in denying it; he could check on it in an instant. 'I'll talk to you Monday.' She put the phone down as gently as she could, and sat, chewing on her blue pencil. There was no way out of it; she was going to have to tell Cade Randall that she couldn't pay him after all. She put the pencil down and looked up the number of his hotel. Thank heaven Jay had told her where he was staying.

She thought for a while that the phone in his suite would ring forever. Finally, though, Mr Thornton's high, thin voice answered.

'This is Lesley Allen,' she told him. 'I'd like to speak to Mr Randall.'

'He is out,' the attorney said primly.

'And when are you expecting him to be in?' Lesley asked, wishing that she hadn't told the man off yesterday. He could have been helpful if he chose—but he wasn't choosing to be, and she had only herself to blame.

'Not until this evening. Is there a message?'

Lesley sighed. Evening would be far too late. Cade hadn't had time to cash that cheque yesterday; the banks had been closed by the time he'd left the magazine office. But he would not hold it very long. And if he tried to cash it today, by evening the police would probably be looking for her.

'It's personal. Please tell him I called and that it's very, very urgent that I talk to him. You must know where he is, Mr Thornton. Please get my message to him immediately.'

'I'll see what I can do, Miss Allen.'

Lesley slammed the phone down, knowing that Mr Thornton would go to no extra trouble. If Cade found time to visit a bank today, she was doomed.

And since there was not one thing she could do about it, she told herself firmly, she might as well get to work.

She didn't have much success. By mid-afternoon her head was throbbing, and she snapped at Shelah, who raised an eyebrow and retreated. When the art director paused in the door of Lesley's office after a particularly acrimonious exchange and told Jana, in a voice he intended Lesley to overhear, that the boss was a bitch on wheels today, she pushed everything off the top of her desk into a drawer and told Jana she was going home. Jana looked relieved.

In the hall outside the condo, she tripped over a box of magazines. It looked as if the deliveryman had brought his little Jeep right up to her door and unloaded it. She dragged the box inside and tore it open. A glance at the titles revealed the source; there was a copy of *Monsieur*, in its plain paper wrapper, right on top. She kicked it aside and went straight to the medicine cabinet for the strongest pain-reliever she could find.

It knocked her out, and a couple of hours of sleep made a world of difference in her outlook. Surely when Cade found out that the cheque was uncashable, he'd come looking for an explanation. He'd said something about payment plans; Lesley suspected that he would rather torment her with those than take legal action.

The nap had left her feeling rumpled, so she took a quick shower and put on her favourite red-terry robe. It was floor-length, with long, full sleeves and a tie belt that snuggled her slim waist. She brushed her hair and let it fall loose about her shoulders, curling down around her face.

She was stirring her supper—a thick vegetable chowder that she'd taken out of the freezer—when the doorbell rang. Probably Jay, she thought, turning the heat down under the saucepan. And no matter what he said, she was not going to leave home this evening. She was in the mood to work on her book tonight, and she was going to do it.

It's something of a bus driver's holiday, she told herself, to work on the magazine all day and then moonlight by writing a book. But the work was different, and it relaxed her.

She looked through the peekhole in the door, and a strange combination of fear and relief percolated through her as she saw who stood there, arms folded across his broad chest.

'Well,' Cade said as she opened the door, 'Thornton told me you'd said it was personal. But I didn't expect it to be this personal.' His eyes roved over her body, and Lesley was suddenly very conscious that she had put nothing on under the terry robe.

'It's not,' she snapped. 'I mean, it's private business, and I didn't want to tell Mr Thornton about it. But . . .'

'You didn't invite me here to seduce me?' Cade sounded disappointed. 'And to think I had such high hopes.'

'I didn't invite you here at all,' Lesley pointed out. 'I said I needed to talk to you. I certainly didn't expect you to turn up here.'

'You weren't downstairs in your office where I expected you to be,' he pointed out logically. 'Are we going to talk in the hallway, or may I come in?'

She stepped back and held the door open. He looked around and nodded approvingly. 'I expected you to have something of the sort,' he said. 'Apartment?'

'Condo. I bought it several years ago.' She curled up in a chair, tucking her bare toes under the edge of the robe, and pointed to the couch.

'Do you mind if I take my coat off?' he asked, and didn't wait for her answer. 'It feels a bit formal considering what my hostess is wearing.' He dropped his jacket on the couch, pulled off his tie, and chose a seat directly opposite her, propping his elbows on the arms of the chair, tenting his fingers together so he could rest his chin on them in a judicial pose. 'Where is Jay tonight?'

'I have no idea. He doesn't live here, you know.'

'At least not all of the time, you mean? Why do you live so close to work?'

Lesley shrugged. 'It's handy. I don't have to get a cab or be on the streets if I want to work late at night.'

'I'd think it would be too handy. How do you ever take a day off? Doesn't your staff interrupt you with every minor problem?'

'I don't take many days off.'

He looked disapproving. 'That's not wise, Lesley. Someday you're going to wonder why you wasted all that time when you could have been having fun.'

'It's called making a living, Cade.'

'Take it from someone who used to be compulsive about work, my dear—it's a lot nicer the new way.'

She shrugged again. He could talk that way; he would never have to work again if he chose not to. While she would have to work even harder now, if Josh pushed that loan through.

He was inspecting the living room. 'It's pretty. You should do a feature on it.' He looked around, noticing the warm wood and wicker combination of her furniture, the bright accents, most of them handmade. It had taken months to get the apartment exactly as she wanted it.

'Do you make all the crafts yourself?' He waved a hand at the patchwork quilt that was draped over the balcony rail.

'Most of them,' she admitted grudgingly. 'I try out most of the needlework ideas in the magazine.'

'Bedroom upstairs?'

She nodded reluctantly.

'Nice. It must have cost plenty to furnish this.' He was looking at a designer chair as he spoke, the most expensive piece of her furniture. 'I'm surprised. Jay seems the type who counts cost very carefully in things like this. How did you get him to do it?'

'Why do you assume that he paid for it?' she asked, hanging on to her temper with a thread. 'It's my condo, and I furnished it.'

'But surely he splits the expenses with you. No, perhaps he doesn't,' he added thoughtfully before she had a chance to reply. 'You do realise, Lesley, that Jay is cheap.'

'He's careful with his money.'

'That's what I said. Cheap. He must have been very sorry or very embarrassed—or both—that night, to make him send a whole dozen roses. Just what did he do . . . or not do?'

'I can't understand why you think it's any of your business whether I'm sleeping with Jay or not.'

'Oh, it isn't,' he said cheerfully. 'I'm just trying to figure out what sort of relationship it is, so I'll know where I fit in.'

'You fit in nowhere.'

He ignored the interruption. 'You must be sleeping with Jay. It's the only way I can explain the roses.' He frowned, then his face lit up. 'No, I've got it! The rosos were on sale. That's why he sent white ones when any joker would know that red is your colour. I'd have sent those enormous ones that are so dark red they're almost black. That is a passionate rose, and it suits you perfectly. Of course,' he added confidingly, 'I'd have been sending them for a different reason.'

Lesley uncurled from her chair and started for the kitchen to stir her chowder. 'If you're wondering how many roses it would take to tempt me into your bed, Cade—there aren't enough in the whole city of Chicago.'

He followed her. 'It's a good thing I'm not sensitive to insults, or you'd have hurt my feelings by now.'

'I'll keep trying,' Lesley muttered.

Cade paid no attention. 'If your relationship with Jay is an open one, I'd like to put in my application for the next time you're looking for an extra lover. It's not my favourite role, of course, but I'll take it.'

'It's not an open relationship. I am not looking for a lover. And if I was, you would be the last man I would consider.' She walked around him to get a big soup mug out of the cabinet.

'Does that mean I'm not trying hard enough?'

'It means you can quit anytime. It's a hopeless cause.'

He looked like a scolded puppy for an instant, then his eyes brightened. 'The soup looks good,' he said hopefully. 'I rushed right over when I got your message, and I didn't have time to eat.'

There was nothing she wanted less than to share her supper with him, but there was still the matter of the money to discuss. Perhaps some food would mellow him. 'Why is there always someone in my kitchen begging for handouts? Get yourself a mug.'

He did. 'I don't know why everyone else hangs around, but you told me you were a marvellous cook. I just want to see if you're accurate.' He looked around the kitchen, eyeing the row of Mason jars that lined an open shelf, full of pasta and other staples. Everything was neat, but it was obviously used a great deal.

She filled her mug and put crackers on a plate, then led the way to the dining room where her place was already set. 'The soup spoons are in the top drawer,' she called.

When he came in she was straightening the flowers that surrounded the candle in the centrepiece. 'We should have candlelight,' he decided and dug in his pocket. She caught a glimpse of initials engraved on the gold cigarette lighter as he held the flame to the wick.

'Do you carry a survival kit too?' she asked caustically.

'No. I quit smoking years ago, but it's habit to carry the lighter.'

'I'd forgotten that you smoked.' It was an idle comment that Lesley immediately regretted. The one thing she didn't want to do was remind him of that night they had spent together. He remembered far too much already, and she didn't want to talk about it.

He smiled. 'There are times that I still want a cigarette badly.' His expression dared her to ask for an example.

She ignored the bait and looked through the relish tray till she found the radish she wanted.

'I suppose you made the candle too, Lesley?'

'As a matter of fact, I did.'

'Is there anything that you aren't interested in?'

She stared at him for a long moment. 'Yes, Mr Randall, there is. You.'

The calculated insult glanced off him. 'That's too bad. You'll have to develop an interest in me if you're going to interview me. When are you going to do that, by the way?'

'Not this issue. We already have our conceited male of the month lined up. How long are you going to be in Chicago?'

'I'll stay until Jay decides to lower his price for the magazine.' He tasted his soup and mused, 'You're right, you are a good cook.'

'You are going to buy the *Woman*, then?'

'I didn't say that.'

She ate a few bites, then put down her spoon, uncomfortable with him sitting across the table. 'Isn't Bambi lonely when you're busy? Or isn't she smart enough to get bored?'

He smiled, but didn't answer the questions. 'She went back to New York yesterday.'

'Oh, I suppose in that case you're the one who's lonely.'

'Come on, Lesley. Don't pretend that you don't know why I brought Bambi.'

'I assumed you wanted—to put it delicately—companionship.'

'Don't be sarcastic about Bambi, dear.'

'I'm not your dear!'

He raised an eyebrow. 'Are you getting back on the liberation bandwagon? I merely meant that it doesn't look good—a woman like you being jealous of a woman like her. Bambi has her place . . .'

Lesley's ordinary good sense burned up in fury. 'I am not jealous, damn it! I am infuriated at men like you who think that Bambi only belongs in the bedroom!'

'Would you want her in your office?' he asked mildly.

'That is entirely beside the point. But for every beautiful toy like Bambi, there are dozens of other women who have both good looks and intelligence. And men can't see past the beauty to the brains—they think that any woman with a good figure automatically can't spell.'

'You're over-reacting. I know you can spell—in fact, you're a hell of a writer. What am I supposed to do, pretend that you look like Grandma Moses?'

'No, but . . .'

'Good, because that pretence is beyond my power. I am unable to ignore the fact that I want to go to bed with you, Lesley.'

'And I'm supposed to find that flattering?'

'Don't you?' he asked quietly.

'No! I am a woman with reasonably good looks and a certain amount of intelligence——'

'Don't be modest,' he interrupted. 'You're beautiful and brilliant.'

'But when you talk about sleeping with me . . .'

'I'm glad you know I mean it. When I take you to bed, I'm not going to leave your brain behind, Lesley.'

'You are not going to get me into bed, Cade.' She tried to stare him down, but he just smiled. It was impossible to get under that man's thick skin, she fumed. She stacked her dishes and took them to the kitchen.

'You cooked. I'll wash dishes,' he offered. 'I do have a few domestic talents.'

'There's a dishwasher.' She rinsed the soup mugs and silver and he put them into the dishwasher.

'Would you like coffee?' she asked, forcing herself to be hospitable.

'No, thanks. Since you're not going to seduce me, Lesley, I find myself wondering. What is this very personal matter that you called me over to talk about?'

Lesley braced herself against the sink. He wasn't going to like this, and she was frankly scared of what he might do. But she took a deep breath and asked, 'In case you hadn't already found out, there isn't enough money in my account to cover that cheque I wrote.'

He looked at her without expression for a long moment, then reached for his wallet. 'Do you mean this one?' He dangled it by the corner, just out of her reach.

'It's the only one I gave you,' Lesley snapped. But relief flooded over her. If he still had it, at least the bank wouldn't be looking for her.

'My intuition told me it might be worth far more if I didn't try to cash it just yet.'

'Will you hold it till next week?' It hurt Lesley to say the words. There was nothing she wanted less than to beg for anything.

He frowned. 'What's so miraculous about next week? Is payday coming?'

'No. But I had to get a loan, and it won't be approved till Tuesday.' She crossed her fingers behind her back and prayed that Josh would come through for her.

'So you didn't have the money tucked away as you said you did. I thought it was too good to be true.' He leaned against the counter.

'I do have most of it. I can give you thirty thousand now, if you'll let me write a new cheque.'

He studied the slip of paper and shook his head. 'No, thanks. I'm rather attached to this one. What are you using for security on that big a loan?'

'The condo,' she admitted.

'And do they know that you're trying to quit your job?'

Trust Cade to think of that. 'Why don't you let me worry about getting the loan and paying it back? You'll get the money, don't fret.'

'Oh, I'll get my money's worth, you can be sure.' His voice was silky, and Lesley shivered.

'You aren't going to file charges, are you? I know what I did is a crime, but I really thought I could have the money today.'

'That wasn't what I had in mind. If you landed in

jail, I'd probably never get the money. I had other means in mind.'

'What?' Her voice was tense.

'Oh—I might ask Jay what he thinks I should do.'

'You wouldn't do that.'

'Why wouldn't I? He'd snatch that diamond ring back so fast he'd probably fracture your finger. No explanations necessary—and even if you wanted to give any, he wouldn't be around to listen.'

'Jay wouldn't do that. He loves me.'

Cade shook his head. 'Jay loves the little icicle he thinks you are, Lesley. One hint of scandal and he'll be gone. What do you think he'd say if he walked in tonight and saw you dressed like that, with me here?'

'He would ask why you were here. He'd never believe that . . .' Her voiced trailed off.

'That we were thinking about sleeping together? Yes, he would, Lesley. He's not as trusting as you think. And do you know something? He'd be absolutely right.'

'I'm not thinking any such thing,' she denied. But she couldn't meet his eyes. Just the thought of being in bed with him was making it hard for her to breathe evenly. It's fear that is affecting me this way, she told herself. She certainly couldn't fight him off if he tried to rape her.

He pushed himself slowly away from the counter and came towards her. 'Have you ever showed him what a little wildcat you can be in bed, Lesley? Or are you an icicle there too? Is that what he wants——'

'Stop it.'

He raised an eyebrow. 'But it entertains me to speculate about what you two talk about while you make love. Do you discuss the magazine? Or perhaps I've underestimated Jay. He might be a real dark horse. Tell me, Lesley, is he a better lover than I am?'

'I'll never tell you.'

'There are ways for me to find out,' he said. 'Just how important is he to you, Lesley?'

'He's the man I love. And the man I'm going to

marry. But I don't suppose you think either of those things is important.'

Cade shrugged. 'I never considered marriage to be a necessary institution, that's certain. It seems to tie one down so.'

'And you never liked to be tied down.'

'No. I think it's much nicer when two people are together because they want each other, not because there's a piece of paper on file that conveys ownership.'

'Are you certain that you aren't just afraid of marriage? Afraid that someone might want more from you than you're willing to give? As long as you're not married, you can always run from those demands.'

'Well, I certainly wasn't willing to marry you, as your father——'

'My stepfather,' Lesley corrected coolly.

'—So helpfully suggested. Of course, the circumstances weren't exactly the usual ones for a wedding.'

'I think you'd have been running no matter what the circumstances were.'

'Perhaps you're right, Lesley. But we're really talking about you here. If I tell Jay what I know, you probably won't be married either, because he wouldn't appreciate finding out that his Angel has been intimately acquainted with one Cade Randall.'

'He also wouldn't sell you the magazine.'

'I'd cry for a whole year if I didn't get it,' he mocked. 'Just how much is it worth to you to make sure I don't tell Jay?'

'You've already taken every cent I have, Cade.'

'Then perhaps you should consider your non-cash assets.'

He was so close to her by then that her quick breathing forced her breasts to brush his chest. He had planted a foot on each side of her so that his legs formed a trap, and he tipped her face up to his, one hand firmly holding her chin.

'You see, honey, unless you give me a good reason not to tell Jay, I'm going to be so tempted that I can't promise not to let him in on our little secret.'

'What would you have to gain?'

'What would I have to lose?' he parried. 'It isn't my reputation that's at stake here. I've studied your fiancé, my dear, and he's the sort to whom reputation is everything.' His hand slid idly down over the curve of her hip.

'You don't have the right to treat me this way just because I owed money,' she breathed.

'You underestimate yourself, my dear Lesley. This has nothing to do with money. This is nature. Two people learning about themselves and what they could do to each other . . .'

'I'm not going to go to bed with you. That would just give you more to tell Jay.'

'Brave words.' His voice was muffled as his lips wandered down her throat to the collar of her robe.

She braced her hands on the countertop at her sides. 'Are you going to rape me?'

He threw back his head and laughed. 'Lesley, my darling, you entertain me so. Is that an invitation? I quite understand, you know. That way you could have your cake and eat it—go to bed with me and still be able to tell Jay that it wasn't your idea. It's perfectly ingenious—and it won't work.'

'I don't want to sleep with you.'

Cade brushed a hand down across the front of her robe to the tie belt at her waist and tugged it gently. 'In case it has escaped your notice, I don't exactly have sleeping in mind either.' The robe loosened.

'Don't—please, Cade.'

'Please don't, or please do?' He didn't give her a chance to answer. He cupped her face in his hands and silenced her with his mouth, nibbling gently at her lips, his tongue teasing against her teeth.

Her lips softened involuntarily under his and instantly his tongue was probing, darting.

His hands slid tantalisingly down to her shoulders, then cupped her breasts, lingering gently. The long, slim fingers seemed to burn through the terry. Then, very gently, his hands found their way under the robe and spread it open to bare her breasts to his gaze.

He released her mouth, and her head fell back as if it was too heavy to hold up. He bent his head to her breast, teasing the pink tip with his mouth till she moaned with pleasure.

'Look at me, Lesley,' he demanded. She reluctantly opened her eyes, and he stared into the smoky grey depths. 'Oh, hell,' he muttered. 'Let's at least be comfortable. I'm getting too old to make love in kitchens.' He swung her up into his arms.

As he carried her up the spiral stairs, her brain unfogged and common sense reasserted itself. She was doing exactly what she had been saying all evening that she would never do—she was within moments of being in bed with Cade Randall.

My God, Lesley, she thought, and started to struggle in his arms.

He dropped her in the middle of her bed and stood there watching as she slid off the opposite side, tugging at the belt on her robe.

'Get out!' she told him fiercely. 'I will not be blackmailed into sleeping with you!'

'Is this what blackmail feels like?' he mused. 'Somehow I never expected it to be so much fun. But since you seem to have strong feelings on the subject ...' He strolled down the stairs. He was very much the gentleman of leisure as he knotted his tie with swift, sure hands, and Lesley was uneasily aware that she wasn't forcing him to do anything. He put his jacket on and buttoned it without hurry.

There was also a nagging question, in the very back corner of her mind, about whether she wanted him to leave after all.

His shirt cuffs properly adjusted under the coat sleeves, Cade reached for the doorknob and turned to catch her eye over the railing. 'There is no deadline. You have plenty of time to change your mind.'

'I won't.'

He raised a doubting eyebrow. 'Don't you ever wonder, Lesley? Aren't you just the tiniest bit curious about what happened to us that night? It could have been a fluke, you know, but don't you want to find out if the world really does rock when we make love?'

'No. Not if . . .' She bit her tongue. Why couldn't you just stop with NO, Lesley? she asked herself bitterly.

He seemed to read her mind. 'I'm not trying to blackmail you, my dear. I've already decided what I'm going to do with that cheque, and it has nothing to do with the question of whether you sleep with me. I won't cash it.'

'What are you going to do—frame it as a souvenir of the past?' she asked stiffly.

'No. I think I'll give it to Jay—as a wedding present.' If you don't want him to have it, don't marry him. See you tomorrow!' He tipped an imaginary hat and closed the door behind him.

CHAPTER SIX

TELLING herself that Cade Randall was an expert in seduction didn't help. Lesley was too honest, when the chips were down, to deny what had happened to her. She had wanted to go to bed with him.

'I've got to talk to Jay. It's past time to tell him,' she lectured herself in front of the bathroom mirror. She finished putting on her make-up and went downstairs to her writing room. The little room was bright and cheerful despite the lack of sunshine.

The stack of manuscript on the white-lacquered desk was higher this morning; all the tension Cade had left her with last night had been put to good use, and she had written most of the night away again.

She stared out of the window over the rolling grey water of Lake Michigan. Later in the day it would be brilliant blue, but the early October sun was weak, and the water looked stormy.

Last night had shattered a lot of illusions. She had convinced herself, over the years, that the single night with Cade had been an accident, not a normal part of her personality. Now she wasn't so sure. She shivered and wriggled her shoulders under the black velvet blazer. It felt so cold in the condo today . . .

It had taken so little effort for him to seduce her that night. But Lesley had explained that to herself long ago; she had been a teenager, without a close family, without a father to show her what men were supposed to be like, without boyfriends to teach her about relationships. It was no wonder that she had been a ripe peach ready to fall into the skilled hands of Cade Randall.

And how she had fallen! She found herself blushing at the memories of that night, her initiation into womanhood at the hands of an expert. She had never dreamed that she was capable of uninhibited passion; the few kisses she had experienced before had been merely adolescent fumblings. They had certainly been no preparation for the assault on her senses that Cade's kisses were.

She had been so flattered that Cade Randall found her attractive that she would have done anything he asked. He told her she was pretty, and that she was unusual—she was so young, and yet she knew precisely what she wanted to do with her life. When he had invited her to his hotel suite to talk about her career plans, she hadn't wasted a moment in debate.

They did talk about magazines, and Lesley drank more wine than was good for her. She wasn't drunk— far from it—but she was high, more from the concentrated attention than the alcohol. No man had ever listened to her before, or thought that her views might be important.

When he said, 'I want to make love to you, Lesley,' she had hesitated only an instant. How could something so special be wrong? And when he added, running a gentle finger down her cheek, 'I know it's the first time, my dear, I will not hurt you, I promise,' there was no doubt left in her mind.

He had been gentle. There was fleeting pain, but it was gone so quickly, drowned in oceans of ecstatic pleasure, that she scarcely remembered.

She had awakened the next morning in the circle of his arms, listening dreamily to the sweet words he whispered, and then the hotel manager had knocked on the door of the suite.

Things had happened quickly after that; she was never quite sure how their visitors got in, though she remembered Cade muttering something about never leaving the chain off the door again. The next thing she was really clear about was seeing her stepfather standing on one side of the bed and the hotel manager on the other, with Lesley huddled in a pitiful heap under the blankets. She didn't know quite what would happen, but she knew it was going to be dreadful.

Cade, on the other hand, had been far from losing his composure. He propped himself up with pillows, lit a cigarette, tossed the spent match towards the ashtray, and smoked silently and defiantly while the manager lectured him about proper conduct in a public hotel.

When the manager ran out of breath, Cade stubbed the cigarette out and said calmly, 'If you've finished, I really must hurry, I have another lecture to give tonight, and—my goodness, it's getting on towards noon.' He patted Lesley's head and added, 'Thanks, love, it's been fun. Just what I needed.'

Then her stepfather, who had been miraculously silent until then, exploded. Lesley cowered under the stream of filthy language he directed at Cade, but Cade merely smoked yet another cigarette. His dark brown eyes turned almost black with anger, but that was the only sign that he even heard the words directed at him. When her stepfather had completed his lecture with the demand that Cade marry her, Cade laughed. The words he had spoken were still engraved on Lesley's memory.

'Go ahead and file charges,' he invited. 'Statutory rape will make an interesting court case. Let's face it, man, it isn't going to be my reputation on the block. I haven't any to protect, and frankly, I'd enjoy the renown. Whether Lesley would like being nationally known as the girl who tried to force Cade Randall to marry her—now that's another story.'

She had protested her innocence, but he had laughed. 'The scam didn't work, Lesley, so don't lie about it. Learn from the experience, and be more careful next time who you try .it on.' The laugh wasn't a pretty sound, and he had dressed—unconcerned about his audience—repacked his luggage and left the room before any of them had recovered the power of speech.

Lesley's stepfather had turned on her, then, and told her that a whore wasn't welcome under his roof. He'd suspected her for a long time, he said, but now that he had actually caught her, he wasn't putting up with her any more. If she tried to come back to his house, he would greet her with a shotgun.

She believed him, and she had never again come within a block of his house. Her mother had sneaked her clothes out so Lesley's girlfriends could pick them up, but she wasn't strong enough to defy her husband openly.

So Lesley had rented a room, and increased the hours she worked, and held on ferociously to the college classes that meant there would be a future for her. She had always known, after all, that she could depend only on herself.

For a while she blamed Cade. He had instinctively chosen the one way Lesley would respond to, an interest in her career plans. It had been cold and deliberate, and she was determined that he would not hurt her without being wounded himself. In the spring she mailed her demand. And when term was over, she took Cade's money and quietly left town, leaving no one who knew where she was going.

But now Cade had caught up with her, and he was setting out to ruin her life—the peaceful existence she had so carefully built by walling off the events of ten years ago. It had not been just a loan; she knew that, Cade knew that—and soon Jay would probably know it too.

Before she could lose her nerve, Lesley picked up the telephone and dialled Emily Nichols' North Shore mansion. Jay stayed there most of the time; unless he had spent the night at his club he would be having breakfast with Emily just about now.

'He's not here, Miss Allen,' the maid told her. 'He left early this morning.'

The telephone was taken out of the maid's hand. 'Good morning, Lesley,' Emily Nichols said coolly, 'Is there some message I can give to Jay for you?'

'Please, Emily. Ask him to call me at the magazine.'

'Is this business or a personal matter?'

Lesley fumed. 'It's business, of course, Emily.'

'I'm so relieved to hear that. You modern women, always calling a man up at the drop of a hat—don't you understand that men like to be the ones who do the calling?'

'I'm not asking him for a date, Emily,' Lesley said dryly, and broke the connection as quickly as she decently could. Thank God Cade didn't know about Jay's mother, she thought, or . . .

Even thinking about it brought back the throbbing headache that had haunted her for the last three days. She took an aspirin and went to work.

She'd been at her desk for just a few minutes when Jana tapped on the door. 'These were just delivered, Lesley,' she said, and set a crystal vase on the corner of the desk. Her voice was frankly curious. 'But there's no card.'

Lesley tossed her pen down and stared at the three dark-red roses, their velvet petals flecked with water-drops, that nodded to her from the crystal vase. Of course there is no card, she thought. I really ought to shred them and send the pieces down to Cade's hotel . . .

She reached for the vase, intending to do exactly that. But Jana was still standing there, curiosity eating her up, and then the fragrance of the roses caught Lesley's nose. She stroked one of the soft petals against her cheek. It isn't the roses' fault that it was Cade who sent them, she thought. It would be a shame to destroy anything so beautiful.

'I wish I had a secret admirer,' Jana said enviously. 'Oh, I almost forgot. Your pictures of Derek Stone are back from the lab.'

Lesley reached for the folder and spread the big glossy prints out on her drawing board. Wide, innocent blue eyes stared at her from every picture. No wonder women fell in love with that face, she thought. He was stunningly handsome. But once you got beyond the face . . .

'It's time for the staff meeting.' Shelah breezed in

from her office. 'Roses again? What have you been doing to become so popular, Lesley? Did you take my advice and seduce somebody?' She didn't notice that Lesley squirmed uncomfortably. Shelah was already bending over the photographs. 'Oh, my God, how handsome can a man get? You're really a super photographer, too, Lesley—but then even I couldn't fail with material like this to work with. This one is definitely cover quality.'

She tossed a print atop the pile. Lesley had to agree; Derek Stone's eyes were mischievously crinkled and his hair was charmingly disarranged by a random breeze as he looked into the camera. The readers would adore it.

'It'll be the closest we've come to a sell-out issue in months,' Shelah predicted. 'And if we follow it next month with Cade Randall we can do it twice in a row.'

'I hope it doesn't come to that.'

'Why not? He's going to be the new owner by then, isn't he?'

'I wouldn't bet my next pay-cheque on it, Shelah.'

Shelah shrugged. 'In any case, he'd be a good draw at the supermarket counters. And if he's willing . . .'

'Next month is the Christmas issue, and the cover is already done, remember? What do you want to do, dress Cade up as Santa Claus?'

'No,' Shelah mused. 'But if someone wants to tuck him into my Christmas stocking, I'd be delighted to unwrap him.'

Lesley didn't bother to answer that one. 'If you'd run a true interview with Cade, it would turn off half of our readers—the half that objects to kitten suits in advertisements.'

Shelah shrugged. 'He's smart enough to keep it to himself if that's how he feels, Les.'

Lesley didn't want to argue the point. 'Let's get the staff meeting started.'

Most of the *Woman*'s staff was gathered around a corner of the conference table, and the noise level in the room was higher than Lesley had ever heard it before.

She looked around in amazement. Usually they had to go and hunt down the necessary staff to hold a meeting, but today everyone was present.

Then she saw that it was Cade Randall who sat on the corner of the table, in the vortex of the excited babble, fielding questions about himself, the Randall Group, the *Woman*.

Jay came across the room to her, beaming. 'Cade wanted to tour the offices, so we're going to start by sitting in on the staff meeting, Angel.'

'He's had the tour, Jay. I gave it to him myself. And are you sure it's wise to bring outsiders into this kind of meeting? After all, he doesn't own the magazine yet, and we discuss some sensitive material.'

Jay's face fell. 'I hadn't thought of that, Angel.' But he brightened quickly. 'Cade knows what he's doing. He won't breathe a word of what he hears here.'

Lesley wasn't as willing to bet, but Jay was still the boss. She could hardly kick the owner of the magazine out of her staff meeting, and as long as he stayed, so could his guest.

So she made her way through the crowd around Cade until she reached her chair at the head of the table, put her folders down, and tapped her pen patiently on the desk until the conversation died and everyone sat down. Cade took the chair on Lesley's right. She concentrated fiercely on her agenda so she didn't have to admit that he was there.

'Let's make this quick so no one has to miss lunch, all right?' she asked. There was a grateful murmur around the room. 'You've all met Mr Randall by now, I believe? Then let's get down to business. Monday is deadline; everything has to be on the four o'clock flight from O'Hare to get to the printer on time.' She pulled a mock-up of the table of contents out of her folder and started down the list with a manicured fingernail. 'The cover story is mine. It just needs finishing touches. The cover photo has been selected, courtesy of Shelah . . .'

Shelah shrugged. 'When it comes to men, I always pick winners.'

'She says it's going to be a sell-out issue. Now for the departments.'

Most of them were already working up to six months ahead, their work on the current issue long since done. The art director, however, was still struggling to reconcile his concept of winter fashion with Lesley's. They wrangled over his views every month, and Lesley was getting tired of the quarrel.

'It will be done this afternoon,' he promised.

'My way, or yours?' she questioned.

'Yours,' he sighed, with a forlorn wave of his hand.

'Be certain I see it by three o'clock,' Lesley warned. 'Now for the columns.'

Shelah sat up straight. 'Our favourite paediatrician will bring in his first column by the middle of next month. He agreed to standard terms—six months trial, all of that stuff.'

Lesley wondered if Shelah had gone to bed with the man after all. Lesley had hoped to talk him into the column by the start of the new year. And she had expected that he'd want much more than the usual starting columnist. She hoped Cade had noticed, and decided that she would bring Shelah to his attention, whatever it took.

'However,' Shelah continued, 'our lovely advice columnist is still holding out. She's written her columns through to the December issue. But that ends her contract, and she is determined not to continue unless she gets double the salary.'

Jay shook his head. 'I can't see that she's worth what she's getting now.'

'I thought you were going to fire her, Shelah,' Lesley murmured.

'I gave her the benefit of the doubt, and you one more chance to change your mind, Lesley. This month she gets the axe, right?' Shelah made a slitting motion across her throat.

'Right,' Jay agreed.

'Then that brings up another problem, Mr Nichols,'

Shelah pointed out. 'In fact, two problems. I'll bet a dollar right now that our columnist will never be replaced, and that Lesley or I—probably Lesley—will end up writing the column. I'm positive that she can advise anyone about anything, but she's overworked now. That's problem number one—we're short-staffed and Lesley is taking up the slack.'

'Shelah, this is not the place . . .' Lesley interrupted.

Cade was silent and absolutely relaxed in the chair beside her, but Lesley could feel his concentration.

Shelah ignored her and plunged on. 'Problem number two is that even with a shortage of people we're cramped into too small a space here.' She raised a hand and started to tick off points on her fingers. 'We don't have room to test appliances if they're larger than a toaster. We desperately need a film lab—it's taking too long to get our prints back. The conference room doubles as a dining room . . .' She looked Jay squarely in the eyes. 'I can go on, if you'd like.'

Jay was squirming in his chair. 'Put it in a report, Miss Evans, and I'll take it under consideration. You have to remember that office space in this area is very expensive. We are on the Magnificent Mile, after all.'

Shelah got the last word. 'Then perhaps we should move.' She sat back in her chair, disgusted. Her eyes met Lesley's, and as plainly as if she had said the words, Lesley could see what she was thinking—that a report was as far as the matter would ever go.

Cade took the pen out of Lesley's hand and scribbled something in the margin of her agenda. Then he replaced the pen, his hand caressing as he closed her fingers around it.

Lesley moved quickly to the next subject, before the subject of office space caused a riot. Nearly everyone felt the same as Shelah did, and Lesley didn't want bloodshed at a staff meeting.

It was several minutes later before she could take her attention off the meeting to read Cade's scribbled message. The scrawl was difficult to decipher, but she finally made it out. 'Jay Nichols is so conservative he wears a vest with his pyjamas,' he had written.

She listened patiently to the discussion and wrote her own note back—'Being conservative does not mean he's next door to being dead.'

Cade raised an eyebrow and wrote back, 'How did he get involved with a magazine, anyway? It's not his style.'

Lesley looked over the agenda. 'That takes care of everything. Regular meeting next Friday. Oh, and Monday afternoon, as soon as the messenger leaves with the package, the cook-off will begin in the test kitchens. Bring your aprons and your appetites.'

Under the cover of conversation and chairs sliding, Lesley said, 'I've always thought that Jay's father won the *Woman* in a poker game.'

'That's interesting. I wonder if Jay plays poker,' Cade mused.

'He wouldn't put the *Woman* up as a stake.'

'I didn't think he would. You realise, don't you, that it is the only asset he has left?'

Trust Cade to know, she thought. He probably knew more about Jay Nichols than Jay himself did.

Cade continued thoughtfully, 'I wonder if he'd be interested in playing for this cheque I took. It isn't worth much to me, but he might find it very ... Interesting meeting, Jay, Lesley runs a tight ship.'

Jay was puffed up with pride. 'Shall we take the tour now, Cade? Will you have time for lunch after we've finished, Lesley?'

She debated her answer. If Cade was going, she'd rather skip lunch entirely than expose herself to any more sly comments.

'Sorry I can't join you, Jay,' Cade said. 'Thornton says he needs my full attention this afternoon.'

'I'd be glad to have lunch, Jay.'

Cade's smile as he turned to follow Jay out of the conference room told her that she hadn't fooled him. Lesley didn't care. At least it would be a chance to talk to Jay.

Shelah was waiting in her office, sniffing the roses. 'Jana tells me you have a secret admirer,' she said. 'But I'll bet I know who they come from.'

'Oh? Who?'

'Derek Stone. He's in town now—I saw it in the morning paper. He's opening a new nightclub act this weekend.' She took a last deep breath of the roses' heady fragrance and stood up. 'Let me have your list again, Lesley. It looked to me as if you had enough on there to take all weekend.'

'It isn't bad. If I work late tonight, and then put in a few hours tomorrow and Sunday . . .'

'How about letting me do some of it so you can take a weekend off? What are you going to do if—heaven forbid—you actually marry Jay Nichols? You won't be able to work twenty hours a day then.'

'Jay understands how important the magazine is to me.'

'If he does, he's more understanding than ninety per cent of husbands. Which, come to think of it, wouldn't be a bad feature for the magazine. How understanding husbands are, compared to five years ago.' She thought about it for a minute.

'What are you going to do? Run a reader survey?'

'Probably. What I don't believe is you, Lesley. If you really loved that guy, you wouldn't be putting in the killing hours you are. You'd want to spend a little time with him. Tell me, when was the last time the two of you had an evening alone? No cocktail parties, no guests—just the two of you?'

'A couple of weeks,' Lesley admitted. 'But we're going to have lunch today.'

'That doesn't count. I've had lunch with you, and your mind never leaves your desk. You see, honey, if you want my opinion . . .' She sat down on the stool beside the drawing board and shook a finger at Lesley.

'I don't.'

Shelah ignored her. 'I don't think you love Jay. I think you want to be married so you're not alone anymore, but you don't want anyone around who will interfere with your workaholic habits. That's why you chose Jay.'

'If the psycho-analysis is over . . .'

'If you loved him, Lesley, you wouldn't be able to wait till you could be Mrs Jay Nichols. Instead, you've been putting off that wedding for a year now.'

'I've been busy. If it pleases you, I'm going to shop for a gown next week. Jay wants a white wedding.'

'Big deal. I can see it now—you're going to walk through the boutiques and decide that nothing appeals to you. I could understand the lack of hurry if you were sleeping with him, but you're not even doing that.'

'You do seem to know a lot about my life, Shelah.'

'Someday you're going to meet THE man, Lesley. And then you will quit your job without a backward glance. You'll be in his bed whether you're wearing a ring or not, and you'll be in such a hurry to get married you won't have time to shop for a wedding gown. So there!'

'Have you said everything you came in for, Shelah?'

'Almost.' She took Lesley's list out of her hand and started to rewrite it on two slips of Lesley's personalised stationery. Before she was finished, Jay and Cade came in. Shelah transferred the last item and said, 'Mr Nichols, Lesley's taking Sunday off. All of it, so why don't you take her out to dinner?'

Jay looked offended at the suggestion, but then reconsidered. 'It's not a bad idea, Lesley. Are you ready to go to lunch?'

Lesley meekly took a wide-brimmed black hat from her closet, thinking that she would like to shove it down Shelah's throat. But instead she adjusted the wide hatband that matched her dress, and said, 'Shelah, why don't you entertain Mr Randall till his appointment time?' It wasn't the kind of revenge she'd like to take on Shelah; the girl would no doubt enjoy a few minutes of flirting with the notorious Mr Randall. But it was all for the good of the magazine, and if Shelah didn't get the editor's job, Lesley hated to think of what might happen to the *Woman*.

'Kara will be waiting,' Jay fussed as they crossed the lobby. 'She isn't going to be pleased.'

Neither am I, Lesley thought. 'Kara is meeting us for lunch?'

'Yes, I thought you girls would like a chance to get to know each other better, without Mother around.'

The same way I'd like to get better acquainted with a sabre-toothed tiger, Lesley thought. Then she sighed. After all, Kara was Jay's daughter, and even if she lived in Paris most of the year, Lesley would have to learn to be civil to the child. She didn't expect Kara to make it easy.

'Tomorrow is her birthday, you know,' Jay reminded. 'Seventeen years old. It's hard to believe. What do you think I should get for her?'

'Why don't you ask her what she'd like? I don't know the girl well enough to have any ideas.'

'Well, I have reservations for everyone at The French Confection for dinner tomorrow. Do you mind if we take a cab to lunch? The Mercedes is in the parking ramp, and if I take it out I'll never find another place to park.'

Lesley put her hand atop her hat to keep it from blowing off. Her eyes were wide and dark beneath the black brim. 'Everyone is coming to dinner?' she asked with forboding.

'Mother and Kara and you and me, I thought I'd ask Cade if he'd like to join us, and . . .'

'I have to work, Jay. Monday is deadline.'

'The child has one birthday a year, Angel, and this is the first one she's spent in Chicago in three years.'

'And she wants to spend it with you, Jay. Not me.'

'You're going to be her stepmother.'

'I'm certain she'd be more comfortable if I wasn't there.'

'Well, I wouldn't be. Our reservations are at eight. We'll pick you up a half-hour early.'

Kara was waiting impatiently in front of the restaurant. 'I feel like a streetwalker, Daddy,' she complained as Jay put a kiss on her cheek. 'I've been standing here forever. You could at least be on time.'

'I'm dreadfully sorry, dear. How about a big piece of blueberry cheesecake, to make up for it?'

'Oh, Daddy, I'm not a child anymore. And cheesecake is so fattening. How about a glass of wine, instead?'

'If you're watching calories . . .' Lesley murmured, and then bit her tongue.

But Kara's attention had wandered. 'Isn't that Derek Stone over there?' she hissed as the hostess ushered them between the crowded tables.

Heads turned to stare as the nearby patrons heard Kara's whisper. Lesley could have sunk through the floor in embarrassment. Then she remembered where unguided hero-worship had led her, at age seventeen, and she said quietly, 'If you'd like, Kara, I'll introduce you.'

'How do you know Derek Stone?' Kara asked sceptically.

'I just spent four days with him in Omaha, where he was doing a nightclub act, so I could interview him for the *Woman*. No wine for me, Jay.'

Jay placed their orders and looked at his watch. 'I forgot to make a phone call. Will you excuse me?'

As soon as he was gone, Kara fixed her wide eyes on Lesley again. 'What's Derek Stone like in the sack, Lesley?'

'I didn't sleep with him, Kara, so I only know what I've read.'

'Come on, you can tell me. I won't say anything to Daddy. Oh, my God, he's coming over here!'

Lesley looked up into brilliant blue eyes as Derek Stone pulled out a chair at their table. 'May I sit down for a moment, Lesley?' He picked up her hand and kissed the back of it. It was one of his most engaging tricks.

'Hello, Derek. When does your club act open?'

'Last night. I was in top form.' Somehow it didn't sound conceited when he said it. 'Are you coming to see me?'

'Perhaps.'

'There's a table reserved for my guests at every performance. I'll give them your name at the office.' His eyes flicked over Kara as he spoke.

Lesley quietly introduced them. 'Kara's father owns *Today's Woman*, Derek.'

'Can we come tomorrow?' Kara breathed. 'It's my birthday, and I know Daddy will bring me.'

Derek laughed indulgently. 'Of course. I'll put your name down, Lesley. Early show or late?'

'Late, please.'

He kissed her hand again. 'I'll see you tomorrow, then.'

Kara looked younger and more excited than Lesley had ever seen her. 'I can't believe it. Now I can tell all my friends.' Then her expression sharpened. 'You must have slept with him, Lesley. He doesn't do that sort of thing for everybody. And if you didn't, there's really something wrong with you.'

'I see you had a visit from a celebrity,' Jay said as he pulled out his chair. In her eagerness to tell her father about Derek Stone, Kara forgot about Lesley.

Lesley ate her lunch in silence. It was unfortunate for Kara, she thought, if the child believed that going to bed was the answer to everything.

Finally Kara ran out of things to say, and Jay turned to Lesley. 'I called Mother, and she said you had something to talk to me about.'

'It wasn't important,' she murmured. She could just see herself sitting in the middle of the restaurant, with Kara hanging on every word, confiding in Jay that she'd written a bad cheque to repay a ten-year-old loan that wasn't really a loan after all but something more like blackmail.

'It sounded important,' Jay disagreed.

Lesley let her gaze rest on Kara for a moment, and Jay nodded his silent understanding.

'Instead of going out Sunday, why don't you come to the condo?' she said. 'I'll fix something simple and we can talk then.'

'Sounds good. The French Confection tomorrow will be all the gourmet food I can handle for a while.'

And it would be less expensive. Lesley squashed the thought, but she had to admit Cade had been right. Jay was cheap.

And there was nothing wrong with being careful with his money, either, she told herself angrily. She felt a little disloyal for even letting herself think it. 'If I have time tomorrow, I'm going to shop for my wedding dress, Jay.' How silly, she thought instantly—saying that to make up for thinking disloyal thoughts.

'I'm glad, Angel. We need to get started planning before Mother changes her mind again.'

Kara's eyes brightened. 'I need a new dress for my birthday, Daddy. If I'm going to a nightclub to see Derek Stone . . .'

Jay laughed indulgently. 'All right, Kara. Perhaps you can trail through the boutiques with Lesley tomorrow and pick out whatever you want.'

Lesley wanted to scream, but she found herself nodding meekly instead.

'He's a pretty important character, isn't he?' Jay asked Kara. 'All you girls fall for Derek Stone. That reminds me, Angel, why don't you schedule that interview with Cade for next month's *Woman*? He'd be a good follow-up for the Stone cover.'

'Two men in a row on the cover of a woman's magazine? The cover story for the next issue is already set up, anyway, Jay. It's Christmas, with the old-fashioned tree, and the pictures are even done. It's a little late to change.'

Jay frowned. 'You have an opportunity here every magazine in the United States would pay for, and you're turning it down? Cade wants to talk to you, and you only. Do the interview, Lesley.'

Lesley sipped her club soda and asked quietly, 'Is that an order?'

'If it has to be, yes.'

'Then I'll do the interview, Jay.' She pushed her chair back. 'If you'll excuse me, I have a deadline to meet.'

CHAPTER SEVEN

SHELAH stood in the door of Lesley's office, her jacket over her arm and concern in her eyes. 'Are you seriously going to stay here and work all night?'

'If it takes all night—yes.' Lesley didn't even look up. She finished the word count on her cover story about Derek Stone and scribbled a note to the printer.

Shelah continued to stand in the doorway, and feeling her assistant's disapproval, Lesley finally put her pencil down. 'To answer the question you're thinking, no, there's nothing more you can do. I'm just catching up on all the work I would have done all week if I hadn't been out of town. Go on home.'

'But I hate to leave you here by yourself at night!'

'Believe me, Shelah, I like being here by myself. It's the only time I can work without interruption.'

'I guess that's a hint, right?'

Lesley nodded. 'How did you and Cade hit it off?'

'All right.' Shelah sounded subdued. 'He'd be a good publisher to work for.'

'Oh? What did you talk about?'

'Things he might do if he buys the *Woman*,' Shelah said vaguely.

'Is he going to promote you?'

'We didn't talk about that. I'll see you Monday, Lesley.' She let the door close gently behind her.

The outer office was already dark, the typewriters hooded, the desktops clear. Over in the corner by the circulation department, the big computer hummed as it busily sorted records, ready for Monday's workday. It, like Lesley, seldom took a day off.

She liked working nights; it was so peaceful, and hours slid by sometimes as she concentrated. She could accomplish in an hour in the evening things that would take all day if she tried to fit them in between interruptions.

But tonight it was difficult to get started. She had slipped away to nap in the afternoon, and returned wearing comfortable faded jeans and a battered sweater so she could stay till the issue was put to bed. But instead of plunging in, she sat staring out of the window for a long time, watching the golden lights of Chicago brighten as the sky dimmed.

It would be the last issue she worked on, she realised, if Cade bought the magazine. And if he'd told Shelah that he had plans for the *Woman*, it seemed certain that the sale would go through. It was no surprise, of course. She had never expected anything else.

No wonder she was dragging her work out tonight, Lesley thought. The *Woman* had been at the centre of her life for almost four years. Being its editor was as natural as breathing, and it would be almost as hard to stop. She didn't want it to end.

But despite Jay's order at lunch today, it would no doubt be Shelah, not Lesley, who interviewed Cade Randall for *Today's Woman*.

She almost regretted missing that opportunity, she thought. It would be fun to question him, to write an interview for once the way it really was . . .

'You already know what he thinks,' she told herself. Her voice was loud in the silent office. With a sudden spirit of mischievousness, she pulled the typewriter stand over beside her desk and inserted a sheet of paper. Cade Randall had never been interviewed like this before, she thought. It was almost a shame that he would never see it.

A long time later she yanked the last sheet out of the roller and tossed it on to her desk. 'You're procrastinating, Lesley,' she told herself firmly. 'Playing word games is fun, but it doesn't get the work done.' So she moved to the drawing board and started in once more. Which pictures of Derek Stone should she use, and where? How big? And, she suddenly remembered, she still had an editorial to write . . .

She would be very careful with her next job, she decided, so that she didn't start to feel responsible for every word in every issue. The *Woman* was her magazine, from cover to cover. But that was not only unhealthy for her, it wasn't good for the magazine either. If she wasn't able to work on an issue—as next month she wouldn't—it would have a totally different character, and to start doing that was to risk subscription cancellations.

She hadn't seen it happening, of course. She had plunged into the *Woman*'s problems headfirst, trying to solve them all at once, and then as she got to know Jay and grew fond of him, she wanted to make everything run smoothly for him. She'd been so efficient as she coped with every problem that now no one else tried. They just brought their troubles to Lesley. No, she'd be more careful with the next job.

It sounded as if someone was trying to kick in the plate glass door. She jerked upright at the drawing board and peered out through the narrow blinds, across the big office, to the entryway.

A shadowy form stood there, hands full of boxes and bags. She recognised the broad shoulders, and debated for a moment about letting him in. But Cade could see her through the blinds, and it was too late to try to hide.

Lesley hunted through her handbag for her key and unlocked the door. 'This is against my better judgment,' she said as she pushed it closed behind him.

'Something told me you'd be here. And I'll bet you haven't eaten, right?'

'I had a nap and a snack this afternoon.'

'That was at least six hours ago.'

Lesley looked at her watch. The time had slipped by faster than she realised. 'I wish you'd stop trying to take care of me, Cade.'

'Someone needs to. You're not doing a very good job of it. Or are you actually trying to lose weight? You're even getting too thin to model for *Monsieur*, you know.'

'Why on earth would I want to be photographed half-naked?'

'Because you look wonderful that way.'

'I'm too old.'

He inspected her from head to foot, his eyes bright. 'Oh, no. Never that. I hope you like Chinese.' He led the way into her office and dropped the jumble of sacks and boxes on her desk.

'Well, I don't have anything against them. Why? Are you hiring some?'

'Chinese food, dummy. It's a good thing I came. I see starvation is affecting your brain. Have a won ton.' She opened her mouth to protest and he popped one in. 'There's sweet-and-sour sauce in here somewhere.' He stripped off his corduroy jacket, looking suddenly younger in the heavy sweater and open-necked shirt, with a gold chain gleaming at his throat.

'Good heavens,' she said, words muffled by the crunchy titbit. 'What did you do, rob a Chinese restaurant?'

'I didn't know what you liked, so I told them to put in a little of everything. Egg roll?'

'Love them. Where's the soy sauce?'

'I'll look. There must be some in here.'

Lesley was investigating a small white box. 'They took you at your word. I can't think of anything I don't see.'

'Are you a chopsticks person?'

'Of course. What point is there in eating Oriental if you don't do it properly?'

He handed her a pair of ivory chopsticks.

'These are hand-painted, Cade. Don't you know about everyday chopsticks?'

'This isn't an everyday occasion. Here's the steamed rice. You do eat rice, don't you?'

'Now and then. Would you mind awfully if I work while I eat?'

'Go ahead. If I expected you to take a break, I wouldn't have brought the food. I'd have carried you off to the Ninety-Fifth instead.'

'You couldn't have got a reservation this late.'

He raised an eyebrow. 'Want to bet?'

'Well—perhaps you could,' Lesley temporised. 'But they wouldn't have let me in. I'm wearing jeans.'

'They'd have pretended not to notice.'

'Touché. You are a powerful person, aren't you?' She dipped her chopsticks into the rice. 'I'd have looked wonderful at a nightclub.'

He was looking appreciatively at the tight jeans. 'Actually, I'm glad to see that you actually let your hair down once in a while. Literally. You look much more comfortable.'

Lesley pushed a lock back over her shoulder and rearranged the pictures of Derek Stone atop the drawing board. She was surprised to find that she was ravenous.

'Good pictures.' Cade was looking over her shoulder. 'You know, I never did understand what women see in men like that.'

Lesley laughed. 'You're joking.'

'I'm absolutely serious. What is so fascinating about Derek Stone?'

'It's the bedroom eyes.' She looked up, and the expression on his face caught at her throat. Her voice was husky as she asked, 'Don't you ever wonder what women see in you—why they fall all over you?'

'Well, I hope they see more intelligence than Derek Stone possesses. Tell me, what do you see in me?'

'I wasn't talking about myself, just women in general.' She turned back to the photographs and began coding each with information for the printer. Why did you have to start this conversation, Lesley? she asked herself.

'You're avoiding the subject. Or perhaps,' he mused, 'it would be easier to discuss it later this evening with the lights out. A great many topics are easier to talk about in bed, in the dark.'

'This is not one of them.'

'What a shame. I'd like to tell you all about your

good points. I don't even care if it's dark.' The wrappings rattled as he looked through them again. 'Here's ginger duck if you want some.'

'I'll pass.'

'I thought you liked everything. Perhaps I should have brought the fried squid after all.'

Lesley shuddered. 'I'll take the duck.' She moved a picture and decided that she had achieved the perfect arrangement.

'Did you and Jay have your little talk?'

'What talk?' she asked absently.

'Come on, dear. The one in which you tearfully unburden yourself of your seamy past, after which he either consoles and forgives, or thunders at you and orders you out of his life. Which was it?'

'Jay is certainly too gentle and loving to order anyone out of his life.'

'Gentle? Jay has all the inner strength of a cream puff. Nauseatingly sweet and sticky and not much use.'

'You and Shelah should get together. She calls him a marshmallow.'

Cade's fingers wandered gently down the length of her hair, brushed out in a wave of blue-black curls over her shoulders, and then traced down her spine over the red sweater. He asked thoughtfully, 'Do you really want to live with a marshmallow, my dear? Or is Jay just a big, fluffy quilt that you think you can wrap yourself up in to hide from the world?'

'I love Jay.'

He moved away from her, walked around the desk to sit down behind it. He propped his feet on the corner of it and folded his hands behind his head. 'Every time you say that, it becomes less convincing. How can you love someone who doesn't have an opinion about anything? You're fire, Lesley. How long do you think Jay could live with you before he'd be only ashes?'

She reached for another egg roll and doused it with soy sauce. 'I'm certain you have some suggestions as to what I should do about it.' She tipped her head back and looked straight at him, a challenge in her eyes.

'That's easy. Ditch Jay and come back to New York with me. Or if you'd rather stay here, I could arrange to spend a lot more time in Chicago.'

She ate the egg roll thoughtfully. 'Are you proposing to me, Cade?'

'Of course not. You know very well that I don't believe in marriage. It's an institution for the insecure.'

'One of those unnecessary complications of life,' she murmured.

'Exactly. We'll stay together just as long as it's right for both of us. That's basically all marriage is anyway, except that it's messier to get out of.'

She turned back to the drawing board. 'No, thanks, Cade. You see, I remember last time, when our undying devotion lasted exactly one night.'

'That was an unusual circumstance. As soon as I left that dinky town, I regretted leaving you behind, you know. It was too bad that your stepfather intervened. If he hadn't, I'd have taken you with me.'

'How flattering. Do you still think it was all a plot we cooked up?'

'No,' he drawled. 'I didn't then, either.'

'But you said . . .'

'If you remember—I had a gun pointed at my head. Figuratively speaking, of course.'

'Well, it would literally have been pointed at me if I'd gone home.' Immediately she regretted saying it. She slid the photographs into a big folder with the cover story, and laid it aside; her hands trembled just a little.

There was an instant of shocked silence. 'Now I really regret not taking you along.'

'Who says I would have come with you?'

There was a laugh in his voice. 'Oh, you would have jumped at the chance.'

'How fortunate for me that I've grown up since then,' Lesley snapped. 'Would you hand me my pica ruler? It's on top of the desk.'

'So you aren't going to come live with me?' He tossed the ruler to her.

'Do I have to spell it out in needlepoint?'

'I'm devastated, Lesley.'

She didn't look up. 'Wonderful. Now would you mind being quiet so I can write my editorial?'

'Do you always cut deadline this close?'

'Of course not. I'm usually a week ahead.'

'I knew it. Workaholic tendencies.'

Lesley put down the ruler and turned to stare at him. 'Is there any way to win an argument with you, Cade?'

'Probably not.'

She bent her head over the legal pad, hearing the rustle of paper as he discarded the cartons they had emptied. Then there was an instant of total silence, and then Cade said, 'So you decided to interview me after all. It would have been nice if you had let me know.'

Lesley gasped. She had forgotten the long imaginary article she had put together off the top of her head. She slid off the tall stool. 'Cade—give me that. Please. It's just a joke.'

He held it out of her reach. 'But I love jokes.'

The desk chair squeaked as he turned it around to face the window, and for a while there was no sound in the office. Lesley sat at the drawing board, doodling on the yellow pad, waiting for him to take her apart. The interview she had made up was not only satirical, it was sometimes vicious.

He put it aside with care and turned to stare at her through narrowed eyes. 'That's excellent, Lesley. You're very good at writing fiction—first cheques, and now interviews. Are you branching out?'

'I was just letting off some steam, Cade . . .'

'I hope you plan to publish it. I won't have to buy the magazine, then—the court will turn it over to me to pay the libel damages.' He folded the sheaf of paper carefully and put it in an inside pocket.

'Cade, please give it to me so I can destroy it.'

'Oh, no. I'm going to keep it as a souvenir.'

It was more likely that the interview would show up in Jay's mail someday with her by-line attached, Lesley thought despairingly. Sometimes she was so idiotic she could just kick herself.

But there was no point in arguing with him. Cade wouldn't give it up, and she certainly couldn't take it from him by force.

'For your information, Lesley, I do not oppose sex-education. I do not believe that all feminists are gay, and I have read the entire text of the Equal Rights Amendment; I know quite well that it says nothing about room-mates or public rest-rooms.'

'But you do think that men should have jobs and women should have men.'

'Most women who have what they call equality have climbed down from the level they were at.'

'Perhaps they didn't like it on that pedestal! Men get commissions—women get minimum wages.'

'What about alimony?' he countered. 'How many men get it? Come to that, how many men get to keep the kids after a divorce?'

'How many want to? Did you know that almost half of divorced fathers never pay any support for their kids?'

'Then of course there are those of us who paid support when there were no kids,' Cade drawled.

Suddenly silenced, Lesley stared at her clenched hands. Then she picked up her pencil again and turned her back on him.

She tried to scrape up an editorial, but her mind was spinning. She scribbled trial sentences one after another, scratching them out as soon as they were written. The click of chopsticks as Cade investigated the remains of the food was the only sound in the office.

But the verbal victory seemed to soothe him. A few minutes later his voice was calm and even friendly as he said, 'I got an interesting telephone call today.'

She wadded up another try at a lead paragraph and tossed it towards the wastebasket. 'Bambi's finally learned how to dial long-distance, right?'

'Why must you be nasty about Bambi? As a matter of fact, the call was from one of your advertisers. Someone has been paying attention to the amount of time I'm spending in Chicago, and he wanted to know if there was any truth to the rumours that I'm buying *Today's Woman*.'

'What did you tell him?'

'I said no, I was just hanging around and trying to buy you.'

She wheeled around. 'Cade, you rotten son of a . . .'

He was laughing, holding up his hands to ward her off. 'I'm only teasing, Lesley!'

'That's not funny. I suppose he thinks that the *Woman* is going to become a female version of *Monsieur*?'

'I suspect you're right. He threatened to pull out his diaper ads if I put in one single cigarette or beer ad.'

'Are you going to?'

'Why shouldn't I? A great many of your readers smoke, and the tobacco industry is willing to pay a premium price for those spots. It shouldn't come as a surprise to you.'

'But we've always prided ourselves on checking out every ad and not promoting anything that might be harmful—or that our readers wouldn't want their children to see.'

'Excellent point, Lesley,' he drawled. 'But who's going to stand up for your views if you leave?'

'That's why you should promote Shelah Evans. She's the best assistant I've ever had.'

'I suspected that was what you had in mind today when you pushed her at me. As long as your organisations stays in place, you will still have a voice in the editorial decisions. Right?'

Lesley ignored the question. 'What did you think of her?'

'She's a realist, Lesley. I don't doubt that she's good, but you're expecting too much when you think she should be as idealistic as you are.'

'You make standing up for what you believe in sound like a bad thing,' Lesley argued. 'What's wrong with being idealistic?'

'Then if I buy the *Woman*, why don't you stick around and see what happens? Keep me from running it into the ground, if you will.'

'I'd sooner die.'

He raised an eyebrow. 'Melodrama, Lesley? I would never have expected it of you. What are you going to do if I don't buy the *Woman*?' he asked thoughtfully.

'Before or after my long sigh of relief?'

'If I don't buy it, Jay's going to lose it.'

She wheeled around on the stool. 'Do you mean he'd shut it down? He wouldn't do that. It would be stupid.'

He looked over his shoulder. 'Jay's no dummy, but that wasn't what I meant. I was talking about a little problem called bankruptcy.'

'Jay isn't bankrupt. The magazine is making money,' Lesley protested.

'At the moment,' he pointed out, 'and only because of the stringent economy you've practised in the last two years.'

'Is there something wrong with economy?'

'No, but you've delayed necessary expansion. Now Jay's got a dilemma. If he keeps the magazine, he's going to have to start pouring money into it—more staff, a move to larger quarters, a bigger budget if it's going to remain competitive. And Jay can't afford to own a magazine that takes a loss. His resources have been drained.'

'You're guessing.' Lesley's voice held a note of relief. He couldn't know what he was talking about. Jay wasn't poor, after all. Cade made it sound as if Jay was down to his last dime.

'That's right,' he admitted cheerfully. 'I am guessing. Jay hasn't been confiding in me over his breakfast grapefruit. But it's plainly visible to anyone who is looking.'

'But the *Woman* is worth millions,' Lesley protested.

'Only if someone wants to buy it. It's not exactly a liquid asset.' He looked her over curiously. 'Don't you know what condition Jay's finances are in, Lesley?'

'If anyone does, I'm certain it's you,' she said bitterly.

Cade smiled. 'Thanks for the compliment. It works like this. Joyce still gets thirty cents of every dollar Jay makes, regardless of where it comes from. And he pays the taxes on it out of his share.'

Lesley shook her head. 'That can't be true. She gets another lump sum payment this year, but . . .'

'You obviously haven't read the divorce decree, as I have. Jay expected to have inherited his mother's money by now, or he wouldn't have agreed to pay Joyce five million this year.'

'Five million dollars?' Lesley's voice was a whisper.

'That's right. See why I'm constitutionally opposed to marriage? It's always associated with divorce, and those things are murderously expensive. If Jay sells the *Woman*, Joyce gets five million plus thirty per cent. After taxes, he'll still have a few million to invest, and Joyce will continue to get almost a third of his income till the day she dies. If he doesn't sell the magazine, there is no way in hell that he can make that lump-sum payment. It's as simple as that.'

'I don't believe you.'

'Ask Jay. I'll bet you anything you like that I'm right.'

'Even if it's true, Cade, she wouldn't force him into bankruptcy.'

'I would bet on that one, too. Joyce has no reason to be generous.' He watched her for a few minutes, studying the play of emotions across the lovely face. 'What kind of stakes would you care to set, Lesley, dear? What about double or nothing on that cheque of yours?'

She shook her head. 'It can't be true.'

'Jay might just sign the *Woman* over to her, to keep the roof from falling in,' he speculated. 'Of course, your job wouldn't be worth much then.'

Lesley didn't comment. She found it hard to believe him, but Cade had no reason to lie. All she had to do was ask Jay.

'If I were Jay,' Cade commented, 'I'd spend my last dime and file a malpractice suit against the attorney that agreed to that awful settlement.'

'If you were Jay, you wouldn't have been married in the first place.'

'That's true.' He propped his feet on the desk again and dug his hands into his pockets.

'Mr Thornton must have enjoyed dragging out all of the details, right down to rummaging through the divorce settlement.' Her voice was bitter.

'He's handy to have around sometimes,' Cade admitted. 'You wouldn't think to look at him that he could be relentless, would you? Once in a while he goes off track, though.'

'Why does that sound like a warning?'

'Oh, Thornton thinks he was right about you after all, Lesley. He says your story doesn't sound true, so he's searching all over Illinois for a trace of a baby you might have abandoned nine years ago. I tried to tell him not to bother, but he's something of a bloodhound, and he thinks he's on your trail.'

'He's wasting his time.'

'You injured his professional pride, Lesley. Thornton doesn't like it when anyone tries to make a fool of him, and so far you're the only one who has ever succeeded.'

Lesley picked up her pencil, but her hand was shaking.

'He's already decided that you didn't arrange a foster home or anything because you no longer have contact with the child.'

'How did he come to that conclusion?'

'He's positive that if you knew where the kid was, you'd have sent a cheque for her birthday at least once, or charged some toys or children's clothes on your credit cards. But there's nothing.'

She was startled. 'How did he get my cancelled cheques and credit card vouchers?'

'Once your name is in a computer, honey, you're fair game for the Thorntons of this world.'

'And Mr Thornton has decided this mythical child is a girl, hmmm?'

'Did I say that?'

'You said something about sending gifts on her birthday,' Lesley reminded.

'Oh. That's my assumption, not Thornton's. He never assumes anything.'

'How interesting that you've imagined a daughter. I'm sure there are Freudian implications there somewhere.'

'Isn't it fascinating? I always thought it would be a girl. You know, Lesley, I never liked children, but over the years I've thought a lot about her. Wondered where she was—what she looked like—even what her name was.'

'How touching.' Her tone was sarcastic.

'I even regretted sometimes that I paid you off. When you took that money, you signed away any rights to future support, but I gave up something too, you know. I came to regret not knowing my daughter.'

'What a pity I didn't know that. I could have held you up at least once more,' Lesley mused.

'I don't suppose there's any use asking what you would have named our child.'

Lesley shrugged. 'I never gave it a thought, Cade. After all, there was no need—remember? And I'm paying back the money, so you can just forget the whole thing. We're even.'

He stayed in the chair, leaning back, indolent. 'We will be even, my dear, when I say we are.'

'You'll have the money next week, just as soon as my loan goes through.'

'You're very certain it will. I, on the other hand, am not so sure. Your banker might be very interested in your plans to quit your job.'

'You wouldn't tell him that. If you mess up my loan I'll never be able to pay you . . .' Her voice dwindled as she thought of the implications.

He reached for his wallet and took out her cheque. 'Somehow, I don't think I'd miss having the cash,' he murmured, studying it. 'Of course you could hurry up and marry Jay. The bank would consider you a much better risk then.'

'You said you'd give him the cheque.'

'I probably would.' He put the damning slip of paper carefully back into his wallet. 'It's my evil tendencies, you know. I just can't seem to control myself sometimes. And if you married Jay, I probably wouldn't buy the magazine either. I'd be so heartbroken at losing you that I couldn't bear to have a reminder.'

'And you think I write fiction,' she jeered. 'You're getting good at it yourself. You've never let sentiment get in your way, Cade. If you want the *Woman*, you'll buy it.'

'Oh, it's a tempting purchase, I'll admit it. But I could turn it down without losing a moment's sleep. What would you do to make it worth my while, Lesley? Is Jay willing to make you part of the bait?'

'Why don't you ask him? If he's in such dire financial straits, he may not be able to afford me.'

She had captured his interest. 'But I can afford you, Lesley. You can always . . .'

'I know. Come to New York and live with you, until you get tired of me. Am I really worth that much money to you?'

'I'm prepared to be very generous. Far more than Jay can be.'

'It doesn't sound to me as if there is much difference between that and walking the streets, Cade. It's still prostitution, even if it is better paid.'

He shrugged. 'Whenever you decide what it's worth to you for me to buy the magazine, let me know. I can wait a long time.' He looked thoughtful. 'I'm not sure how long Jay has. You might want to ask him when that five million dollars has to be paid. Joyce isn't known for her patience.' He stood up. 'I'll see you tomorrow sometime. Do I get a goodnight kiss?'

CHAPTER EIGHT

KARA was seventeen trying to look twenty-five today, Lesley thought as she sat across the table from the girl. She had invited her future stepdaughter to lunch, hoping that Jay was right—perhaps if they just got to know each other, they would discover some common interests.

But so far all Lesley had discovered was a headache and a bone-deep gratitude that Kara spent eleven months of the year on the far side of the Atlantic.

She stirred her coffee and asked, 'Where shall we start, Kara?'

'Lord and Taylor,' Kara responded instantly. 'I've got Grandmère's credit card, and she told me to buy whatever I wanted for school. Then I want to go down that whole row of boutiques and buy my dress for tonight. It has to be something special since we're going to see Derek Stone. And we have to go to Christian Bernard, because Daddy told me I could choose my own birthday gift there. I think I want an opal ring, with a little diamond on each side.'

And no doubt Daddy expects me to exercise some control, Lesley thought wearily. She could cheerfully strangle Jay today.

'Well, let's get started,' she said, trying to put on a smile. Shopping was her least-favourite activity anyway; Lesley bought clothes twice a year, colour-coordinated everything, and seldom set foot in a shop at any other time. It was bad enough to be looking for a wedding gown that she didn't want to wear. But to have an adolescent trailing along, shopping for school clothes— she shuddered at the thought.

'What's in that big package you're carrying?' Kara asked curiously as they left the restaurant and came out into the bustle of shoppers in the gleaming glass and steel core of Water Tower Place.

Lesley shifted the manila envelope to her other hand. 'Just something I have to drop off today.' She was discouraged again by the book manuscript. After all the work of the past few days, she was ready to give up on it entirely. Yet somewhere in the back of her mind lingered the conviction that the book was good, that it could be made into something that would sell. But she was no longer sure if she was the one to do it. So she had bundled the manuscript together and called Bob Merrill to ask if he would look it over. After all, he was an agent; he could tell her whether she was wasting her time.

'The envelope says "manuscript" on it,' Kara observed.

Lesley nodded.

'Are you trying out for a movie or something?'

'It isn't that kind of script, Kara. Would you mind if we drop it off first? The office is just down the street, and it's too heavy to carry.' And, frankly, the sooner it was out of Kara's sight, the sooner she would forget it. The last thing Lesley wanted right now was to have Jay start asking questions.

Bob's office was on the third floor of an old brownstone and when faced with climbing the stairs to the tiny two-room suite Kara decided to wait downstairs for which Lesley was grateful. She had been wondering how she was going to manage to talk to Bob in private.

He had the phone at his ear when she pushed the door open, but he waved to her to come on in. 'Well, if you'd rather have the champagne brunch . . .' he told his caller, and paused. 'All right, I'll meet you at the Haymarket at noon. We'll hash it out then. I've got some good stuff for you.' He slammed the phone down and said, 'Editors! I can't make a living without them, but I'd cheerfully send some of them to eternal fire.'

She handed him the package. 'Thanks for meeting me here on Saturday, Bob.'

'No problem. I would have been here anyway, trying to make a living. So the opus is finished, Lesley?' He pulled it out of the envelope, looked at the cover page, then eyed Lesley with a speculative gleam.

How she had agonised over that title, she thought; if it grabbed Bob's attention, perhaps it had been the right choice after all.

She shook her head. 'It isn't finished by a long shot. But I've lost all perspective, and I need someone to tell me if it's even worth the effort.'

'Well, I can certainly do that. Give me a week or two—I should be able to tell you something by then.'

'Thanks, Bob. I hope it doesn't bore you to tears.'

'I'm not easily bored, or I wouldn't have lasted long in this profession. Thank God I'm past the point of having to read everything that comes in my mail.'

'You don't?'

'No. Most of the unsolicited stuff goes back as soon as my secretary browses the first page. When I was starting out and trying to discover something good in the slush that the postal service brought me, I thought I'd surely die of a caffeine overdose, trying to stay awake on black coffee.'

'I still read everything I get,' Lesley mused.

'Don't bother. If page one isn't enough to hold your attention, how can it grab a reader's?'

She shook her head. 'That sounds reasonable, but I think everything deserves a fair reading.'

'Almost everything I get from unpublished people has already been submitted to a half-dozen editors,' Bob pointed out. 'They read it and said it was no good, and ninety per cent of the time they were right. Now I only handle people with credentials.'

'Thanks for taking me, then.'

'Listen, how good do you think credentials have to be? You put out that darn magazine single-handed every month. And speaking of the *Woman*, I've got a terrific romance novel for you. I can get you first North American serial rights for just . . .'

'Talk to Shelah Evans.' It hurt Lesley's throat to say the words; she had wanted to be the one to run the *Woman's* first full-length book.

Bob sat down on the corner of his desk. 'Aren't you going to stay at the *Woman* when Cade Randall takes over?' Curiosity oozed from his voice.

'Rumour certainly travels fast, doesn't it?'

'Jay gave him an option, you know. There's no keeping negotiations quiet in this town after they reach that stage. So what are you going to do, Lesley?'

'I haven't decided yet.'

'Did you quit? Surely you weren't fired. Or maybe you've been promoted,' he speculated. 'You're certainly good enough—I bet Randall wants you in the home office.'

Well, he wasn't far off, Lesley thought. Just leave out the word 'office' and Bob had hit the nail on the head.

'Is Jay going to move to New York with you?'

'Did I say I was moving?'

'You're no fool, Les. You know what the Randall Group pays its people.'

'Salary isn't everything Bob. And for right now I'm firmly rooted in Chicago.'

'Okay. Have it your way.' He grinned cheekily. 'I'll pretend to be surprised along with the others when you make your announcement.'

Lesley could almost see the wheels turning in Kara's head as she joined her in the spring sunshine. But the girl made no comment.

Shopping with a teenager was everything she had feared. Turning Kara Nichols loose with a Lord and Taylor credit card was like watching a mass murderer on a spree. And Emily Nichols' American Express card should have been smoking from over-use by the time Kara was finished.

Lesley thanked her guardian angel that the girl knew about delivery services; she did not want to stagger back up the street carrying forty boxes and a fox-fur jacket that Kara had insisted would be perfect for skiing in Switzerland next Christmas.

Lesley must have looked quizzical about the jacket.

'Oh, I won't wear it on the slopes, of course.' Kara tossed a hand in the air. 'But there are so many parties, and sometimes I want to go for a walk with a guy. Find a place to be alone, you know.'

The fox fur jacket should be suitably impressive, Lesley thought, especially with Kara's blonde hair. 'Does your mother like to ski?'

'Oh, heavens no, Mother thinks it's ghastly. That's why I go on the school tour.'

'I should think you'd miss being with her at Christmas,' Lesley murmured. She reached out to finger a basic black cocktail dress, layers of tulle floating over an old-fashioned taffeta sheath. It was pretty, but just at present it wouldn't do to even look at the price tag. That second mortgage to pay off—assuming it came through at all—would be pinching her budget for some time to come.

'Not at all. Why should I waste three weeks in Paris in the middle of winter when opening my gifts only takes a few hours? She goes to Cannes, anyway, and she'd hate having to stay in Paris. Are you going to try on that dress?'

'Do you like it?'

'No. It looks like something Grandmère would choose. But it might look good on you. The neckline might even flatter that pointy chin of yours.' Kara studied her companion frankly and added handsomely, 'But you do have nice bones in your face. Mother says that's the most important.'

Lesley thanked her gravely and said, 'If you've finished looking here, perhaps we can go on to the bridal department.'

'All right. Just wait till I tell Mother that I helped choose your wedding dress. She'll have a fit.' She almost skipped with delight, and suddenly she looked much younger than seventeen. Joyce was doing her daughter no favour, Lesley thought sadly, by pushing her into growing up so quickly. She needed a mother's interest far more than she needed a skiing trip.

All the same, she decided, she was damned if she'd let the brat help choose anything. And she was not going to try to fill Kara's need for a female parent. She'd rather try to mother a panther cub.

'Are you really going to wear a formal white gown?' Kara asked doubtingly.

'That's what your father wants.'

'Yes, he told me. But aren't you a little old for white?'

'A bride is never too old to wear white, as long as it's her first wedding. And it is the first time I'm getting married.'

'But it isn't Daddy's,' Kara objected.

'That doesn't matter.'

'I'm surprised at him, actually. Daddy's such a stickler for doing the right thing that I expected he'd have told you not to wear white.'

Despite herself, Lesley felt colour rise in her cheeks.

Kara didn't miss it. 'Do you mean you really are a virgin, Lesley? I didn't think there were any your age left.'

'There are still some people to whom it's important, Kara.'

'I know. Daddy's one of them. I don't understand it,' she said, shaking her head. 'Virginity was a bore.'

'Was?' Lesley asked coolly.

'Yeah. I got rid of mine a long time ago. It was no big deal, after all. Want me to tell you what to expect?'

'No, thanks, Kara.' Sex education from a teenager she didn't need. Lesley didn't know why she was surprised; Kara was not a child, and she had just been Kara's age when Cade ... Let's get that train of thought off the track, Lesley told herself firmly. Sometimes it seemed that Kara had an unholy ability to read her thoughts.

Kara thought it over. 'Doesn't it feel weird to not know what sex is like? I used to wonder a lot, before I tried it. And you even write about it sometimes, and yet you don't have any experience.'

But I do, Lesley thought. And I was taught by an expert . . .

Kara skipped on, apparently realising that Lesley wasn't going to answer. 'Aren't you going to feel strange walking down a long aisle in a train and a veil and all that stuff?'

'Probably. Do you really think weddings are weird, Kara?'

'Oh, no. I want the biggest, fanciest wedding ever. A dance and a sit-down dinner and everything.'

'And a white gown?' Lesley asked drily.

Kara looked amazed that the question had been asked. 'Of course. I just thought that it seems kind of odd for old people to want to make all that fuss.'

'I am twenty-seven, Kara. I do not suffer from rheumatism and I am not looking forward to drawing my pension.'

'Oh, I'm sorry. I didn't really mean to say that you're old.'

'I'm sure you didn't, Kara.'

What was there about wedding gowns that always depressed her, Lesley wondered as she looked around at what seemed acres of organdie and lace and satin. It might be autumn outside, but here in the wedding department it was already spring, and the garden wedding was expected to be at an all-time high next year. Nearly every gown was ruffled and low-necked and covered with fussy embroidery. They were all beautiful, Lesley knew, but they just didn't appeal to her.

Perhaps it was just that she didn't want to walk down the aisle by herself, she thought, and she had no male friend whom she wanted to escort her. If Jay would just be sensible about a small, private wedding, instead of a big affair in that empty, echoing cathedral . . .! She could wear a white wool suit with a catchy little hat; she liked hats, and she looked good in them. A private wedding didn't have to look as if something was being hidden.

She'd talk to Jay again before she tried on dresses. The sudden relief was overwhelming as she turned away from the mirrors and the mannequins.

And if that didn't convince him, she thought, she could always take Cade up on his invitation. The one thing guaranteed about Cade was that he would never ask her to buy a wedding gown.

Derek Stone had a decent voice, but if it hadn't been for his looks he would never have made it as a nightclub act, Lesley decided. She looked around the table and discovered that for the first time ever she and Emily Nichols were in agreement. Whether Emily would admit to it was another question, but she was sitting stiffly upright, the perfect lady refusing to admit that she had found herself in the middle of a bad dream.

Kara, of course, was in heaven; she was hanging on every word Derek Stone sang. She had insisted on a royal blue cocktail dress; instead of giving her the sophistication she longed for, it merely made her look younger and even more spoiled. Lesley thanked heaven once more that at the end of the month Kara would go back to Europe.

Jay sat beside her, looking abstracted. He had hardly said a word all evening, through the gourmet meal at The French Confection and even in the Mercedes on the way to the nightclub.

Of course, Lesley thought, with Kara bubbling over with excitement at meeting her hero, no one else had to supply any conversation.

Jay was too well-bred to show his boredom, but Lesley could see it in the twitch of his fingers on the martini glass. He ordered another drink and leaned towards her, saying under his breath, 'I need to talk to you, Angel.'

'Right now?'

He gestured towards the low stage where coloured lights played over Derek Stone's handsome profile as he belted out a love song. 'Do you mean to say you're enjoying this?'

'Not particularly. But . . .'

'Well, I'm not going to sit here and shout about my business.'

Kara looked at them fiercely across the table. Jay subsided instantly.

'Let's go out to the lobby,' Lesley said. She excused herself and found her way across the dimly lit room, unwilling to wait for Jay to explain to his mother where he was going.

By the time he joined her, she was looking out over the city from the atrium lobby. Derek Stone's band was a murmur in the background instead of the eardrum-threatening roar it had been inside the club. And the air was pleasantly cool against her face. She was wearing jade green tonight, a simple dress with short puffy sleeves and a demure neckline. Not a particularly good choice, Lesley had decided after she bought it, but Emily would approve. Her hair was piled in large curls at her crown, and the only ornaments were the twin diamonds sparkling in her earlobes and the matching stone on her left hand.

Jay looked worried, and very tired, she thought as he crossed the lobby. He was always handsome, especially in dinner clothes. But the last few days seemed to have aged him. It was so dreadfully important to him that Cade buy the magazine. If he didn't, Lesley thought, Jay would be devastated.

'I wanted to talk to you before dinner,' he said, 'but we were late, and with Mother and Kara around . . .'

He didn't have to finish the sentence; everyone knew how impossible it was to have a serious conversation with Emily listening in.

'I spent the day with Cade's people trying to hammer out an agreement,' he said.

'Any luck?'

'We're getting there. We haven't even got to a price

yet; we're still bargaining over details. But late this afternoon Cade threw in another demand.'

Lesley's whole body felt cold. 'What is he asking?'

Jay put his hands on her shoulders and looked down into her worried eyes. 'He wants your contract written into the sale agreement.'

She should have expected something like this, she told herself wearily. Cade wouldn't let her escape so easily. She shook her head. 'I don't want to work for him, Jay.'

'I know, Angel. I don't want you to work either, but if that's the key to selling the magazine . . .'

'Jay, don't you see what he's doing?'

He looked startled. 'You're a valuable person. He wants to have you there during the transition, rather than bring in all of his own people. It's only for a year, Angel.'

'It won't take a year, Jay.' Suddenly she was frightened. Cade wanted her in his bed, and she was terrified that her own body, and her own curiosity, would betray her. If she stayed away from him, she'd be all right. But if she had to work with him for a year . . .

And she was under no illusions. Cade might live in New York, but he'd spend the next year in Chicago if he had any power over her at all. Cade didn't let anything stop him from getting what he wanted. And Lesley didn't think she could hold out that long.

The man was hypnotic. Despite her best intentions, and despite her love for Jay, she'd almost gone to bed with Cade that night—had it only been two days ago? There was something about him that drew her, that made her helpless to resist that undeniable charm.

And he was right. She did wonder sometimes if that night so long ago had been unusual, or if making love with Cade Randall could always cause the universe to grind to a halt.

'If the transition is made in less than a year, I'm sure you'd be free to leave then,' Jay said. 'It isn't as if we've set a wedding date, after all. We can wait.'

'Yesterday you wanted to be married immediately so your mother wouldn't change her mind.'

'Well, we could go ahead, if you like,' Jay said uncertainly. 'I just thought perhaps it would be too much for you all at once, with a wedding and the magazine. We could postpone our honeymoon trip till you've stopped working.'

'Don't you mind, Jay?' Lesley asked fiercely. 'Don't you care that Cade Randall is arranging your life for you? Haven't you even noticed that he's blackmailing you?'

Jay looked horrified. 'Now, Angel—don't say that so loudly. That's a pretty strong word. Of course he wants to keep my best employees there, so the magazine doesn't falter. Whatever else Cade is, he's intelligent.'

'He's smooth,' Lesley said, and the tone of her voice made it sound like a curse.

'Lesley, for God's sake, you've been working there for four years. We're talking about a maximum of one more, and maybe just a few months. What is the matter with you?'

Lesley shook her head. 'You don't know what you're asking.'

'It's the only way he'll buy the magazine, Angel.'

'That should tell you something right there, Jay,' she muttered.

'If he doesn't buy it, I'm done, darling.' His voice was lifeless.

Was it Jay's way of telling her that Cade had been right, that he would be bankrupt if the *Woman* didn't sell?

Jay walked across to the glass wall, his hands deep in his pockets. His shoulders slumped, and his head was bowed.

Lesley could stand no more. What choice did she have? If she held out against the contract arrangement, Cade would just give Jay that cheque. Why, she asked herself again, had she ever been stupid enough to write it? And why did she have to be so vulnerable to a man who didn't hesitate to use blackmail to get what he wanted? Why couldn't she just tell him to go to hell?

Because it would hurt Jay, she told herself, 'All right,' she said finally.

He whirled around. 'You'll do it?' The relief on his face struck at her heart.

'But only as a last resort,' she warned. 'If you can make a deal on everything else, and that's the only thing left holding up the sale, then ...' She swallowed hard. 'Then I'll work for Cade Randall.'

'Of course, Angel. I'm not crazy enough to give up all my bargaining power by telling him right away that you've agreed. He wants the magazine—that much is obvious.'

Not as much as he wants me, Lesley thought morosely. I suppose I should be flattered that he's willing to pay so much for me.

It was intermission when they returned to the nightclub, but the lights were still dim. Lesley was almost to the table before she saw who was sitting there. She drew a deep painful breath and forced herself to meet Cade's gaze without flinching. Jay had told her that he was invited, she remembered. It should have been no surprise.

He rose, the perfect gentleman, and held the chair next to his. Out of the corner of her eye Lesley identified his companion. No Bambi this time, she thought. Beside Cade was Marissa Benton, who had just won an Oscar for a film she had not only starred in, but produced and directed. She was even more gorgeous in person than she looked on the screen.

But she's got one thing in common with Bambi, Lesley thought spitefully; both of them earn a living by taking their clothes off. The fact that Marissa did her undressing on screen didn't change the similarity.

But what was she doing here? She remembered Shelah telling her that Cade had been seen with the woman, but as far as Lesley knew, Marissa had not willingly seen Derek Stone since their bitter divorce a year ago.

'Were you and Jay having a lovers' quarrel?' Cade asked softly as he sat down.

'I don't know what you mean.'

'Jay must have won this round,' he mused. 'He looks much more peaceful than you do. I didn't know the man had it in him.'

As if Cade didn't know what the argument had been about, she thought. She ignored the comment and said hello to the actress.

'Marissa's going to be here for a few days,' Cade said. 'Perhaps you can persuade her to appear in *Today's Woman*.'

'When you own it, Cade, you can give the orders on how to run it,' Lesley muttered. 'In the meantime, I'll take care of it.'

He raised an eyebrow. 'Surely you're not going to cut off that lovely little nose just to spite me, Lesley?'

Derek Stone laid his hand on Lesley's shoulder and leaned down to put a long, possessive kiss on her mouth, 'Lesley, my darling,' he said in that husky tone that made women want to swoon, 'I hope you know that I've been singing just for you.' He glanced around the table. 'And for you, too, Marissa. Long-ago memories have a way of popping up where they're least wanted.'

Marissa sipped her drink, batted long, curly lashes, and said gently, 'I'm touched that you remember me at all, darling. There were always so many women around you that I'm gratified to hear that I stood out from the crowd.'

'Perhaps you could interview them both,' Cade murmured in Lesley's ear. 'It should make—shall we say—a hot issue?'

Trust Cade to keep the pot boiling, Lesley thought. 'Sorry. I didn't bring my notebook.'

'Or if that doesn't meet your standards, you could always interview yourself about your intentions. After the gossip columnist at the next table finishes dissecting Marissa and Derek, she's going to start on you.'

'Why?'

'Because, like Mount Everest, you're there. And the air of mystery about you is such a temptation to rip away.' He raised a hand to brush her cheek, as if to tear away an imaginary veil.

'Keep your hands off me,' she snapped.

'That's good,' Cade said. 'You've got her attention now. Quite a feat it is, to make her forget the quarrelling Stones.'

She turned away just as the waiter set a tall, frosted birthday cake in front of Kara, candles already aflame.

'Very well done,' Cade applauded. 'The air of ignoring me, I mean.' His fingertips brushed across the shoulder of her dress. 'The first thing I'm going to do when you decide to move in with me is throw out about half of your wardrobe. This makes you look just the same age as Kara, and I don't like to rob cradles.'

Lesley concentrated on the flames, wishing that she could consign Cade Randall to eternal residence in them. 'I was exactly the same age as Kara is.'

'You didn't act seventeen in bed,' Cade said smoothly.

'Make your birthday wish, dear,' Emily Nichols urged.

Kara closed her eyes for a moment, then blew the candles out. 'I wished for Derek to sing for me,' she announced.

'And I'm sure he will,' Jay said. 'Mr Stone? Would you . . .'

But Derek was preoccupied. 'You were the one who wanted the open relationship,' he reminded Marissa. 'You announced that you didn't plan to give up your friendships. And then you . . .

Emily Nichols looked as if she was going to have apoplexy.

The waiter set a slice of cake down in front of Lesley. She looked at it with disfavour. Birthday cakes, especially commercially baked ones with thick, heavy frosting, were not her idea of dessert.

'Have you noticed the colour of your future mother-in-law's face?' Cade asked conversationally.

Lesley ignored him.

'If she's this upset about Derek and Marissa, I wonder what she'd say if she knew about you and me?'

Something snapped deep inside Lesley. She turned slowly to face him. 'If you want a scene, Cade,' she said calmly, 'why don't you just try this on for size?' She picked up the slice of cake on its fancy little doily.

The frosting made a lovely smooshing sound as the cake spread out in a wave over Cade's face. It clumped in his eyebrows and smeared down across his tanned cheek as Lesley, with a gentle rotation of her wrist, ground it into his skin.

For an instant no one moved. Marissa Benton's lovely mouth was hanging open, most unattractively. Kara's face was rapt. Emily Nichols sat bolt upright, her lips tight. Jay had put his hands over his face. Derek Stone looked as if he'd been hit by lightning.

Lesley wiped her hand off on a napkin and rose. 'If you will all excuse me?' she said politely.

The silence followed her all the way to the door. But she would have sworn that under his frosting mask, Cade Randall was laughing.

CHAPTER NINE

LESLEY finished slicing cauliflower and laid the small florets out on a paper towel to dry. She stood back and inspected her dinner menu, laid out on the counter top. Steaks ready for the grill, homemade rolls ready to pop into the oven, cauliflower and mushrooms waiting to be dipped into thick batter and deep-fat fried, salads crisping in the refrigerator. It was Jay's favourite menu. She hoped that it would be enough to soothe his anger.

He had still been furious that morning when she had called to see if he was coming for dinner. She understood, of course. Smearing Kara's birthday cake into Cade's face was not what Jay considered to be proper behaviour.

She hadn't let it bother her, though. She'd taken a long, luxurious nap, and a hot shower, and read the entire *Sunday Tribune*, which she hadn't done in weeks. It had been a pleasant, quiet, peaceful day.

'Funny,' Lesley mused as she wiped a spot off the stained-glass door of a cabinet, 'that I never saw Jay lose his temper until this week. And now he's been mad at me almost continuously for five days.'

But that was to be expected. With Cade Randall around, continually stirring up trouble ...

Well, tonight was her chance. She'd feed Jay well, and after he was mellowed, she'd tell him the truth. The whole truth. Once Jay knew everything, Cade's power over her would be gone. And if that ended her engagement, then she would just have to accept that, too.

Obviously she hadn't known Jay as well as she thought she had. Two weeks ago she would have sworn that she knew every important detail about Jay Nichols, the man who was always calm. Now she knew that she had much more to learn.

'And after all,' she said aloud, 'isn't that what marriage is all about? It takes a lifetime to really know a person.'

She glanced at the clock. Now that the messy preparation was done, she'd go put on that slinky black satin blouse and brightly coloured long skirt that Jay liked. He hated to see her in jeans, and she certainly didn't want to get into that argument tonight.

She was halfway up the spiral stairs to her bedroom when the doorbell rang.

'You're early,' she said as she pulled the door open. 'I was just going to change . . .' Her voice trailed off.

'I didn't know you were expecting me,' Cade said cheerfully.

Lesley tried to slam the door, but he inserted a foot into the opening.

'Haven't you ever been told to ask who's outside the door before you open it? I could have been any crook in downtown Chicago.'

'Cade, you're worse than any crook could be. Jay will be here any minute, so would you just go away?'

He looked disappointed. 'I came by to invite you out to dinner.'

'What happened to Marissa?'

'She and Derek patched it up last night. They sang a couple of numbers together and then went back to his hotel like a pair of turtledoves.'

'And poor Cade was rejected again,' Lesley mocked. 'It must injure you dreadfully when you find yourself on the wrong corner of the triangle.'

He nodded. 'That's why I came to you, to have my ego soothed. You're always so gentle about it. I tried to call, but you haven't been answering your phone.'

'I didn't want to talk to anyone.'

'It seems to be reasonable. Are you going to let me come in so I can apologise?'

It took her so much by surprise that she relaxed her hold on the door, and Cade slipped through it. He put a bottle of wine into her hands and locked the door behind him.

'What are you apologising for?'

He shrugged. 'I'm not sure, but I must have done something to make you cover me with cake last night.' He made a grand theatrical gesture. 'My dear Lesley, it breaks my heart to see you unhappy. And so, whatever my sins have been, I . . .'

'Oh, stop it. You know quite well what your sins are.'

He looked injured. 'You didn't let me finish. I stopped by in the hope that we could kiss and make up . . . so to speak.'

'All right. You're sorry for what you said. I'm sorry I smeared frosting on you. Now we're even. Okay? Goodbye.' She tried to usher him towards the door, but he was an immovable object.

'Aren't you going to open the wine? You know, break bread with the enemy and all that.'

'Jay will be here any minute.'

He raised a hand. 'I promise that I'll leave just as soon as Jay gets here.'

'How about a few minutes before, so I can change clothes?'

'Go ahead and get dressed. I can find the wine glasses by myself.' He dropped his dark brown suede jacket over a chair. His shirt, the top buttons open, looked like silk.

Lesley shook her head. 'I'm not that crazy. If I went up to change, and Jay rang the bell, you'd answer it.'

'It would be impolite to ignore it,' he pointed out.

'And you'd convince him that we'd been up in my bedroom together.'

Cade looked horrified. 'Would I do such a thing?'

Lesley led the way to the kitchen and took a corkscrew out of the drawer. 'Here. Make it snappy.'

He expertly drew the cork out of the bottle with a pleasant little pop, and took two gleaming stemmed glasses from the rack. 'To a new start, and a better understanding,' he said as he raised his glass. 'Besides, what's wrong with the clothes you're wearing? You look comfortable and casual.'

Lesley ignored him and put the pan of dinner rolls in the oven.

'Of course, you'd look better wearing no clothes at all,' Cade mused. 'But then, perhaps that's too much to ask.'

The telephone rang at his elbow. 'Want me to answer it?' he asked helpfully.

Lesley reached across him to pick it up.

'At least you're answering the phone now,' Jay said testily.

'What's the matter, Jay?' Then Lesley bit her tongue, for Cade smiled wickedly when he heard the name.

'I can't make it for dinner. I've spent the afternoon with the lawyers, and they want to keep at it till we're done. We may reach an agreement tonight, so . . .'

'I understand.' She tried to dodge Cade, but he lifted her hair up and kissed the nape of her neck, then put his arms around her, pulling her back so that she was leaning against his chest.

'We'll talk later, all right, Angel? I'll stop by the condo when I finish here if it isn't too late.'

'Please do, Jay.' Cade started to nibble her earlobe, and Lesley thought fleetingly about hitting him with the phone. But she hung it up instead.

'Is Jay having a problem?' Cade enquired, sounding only mildly interested. His hands slid from her narrow waist up under her sweater.

She pulled firmly away from him and started to dip mushrooms into the thick batter. 'You should know,' she said over her shoulder as she dropped the first one into the hot oil. 'I'll bet you arranged for the lawyers to work all day Sunday.'

Cade shrugged. 'I can't stick around here indefinitely, you know.'

'Shouldn't you be down there negotiating, too?'

'That's what I pay legal fees for. In any case, whether I make the purchase or not, I have to be back in New York at the end of the week.'

She stood very still, a dripping mushroom in her

hand. Relief, that's what this feeling is, she thought. I didn't expect it to be quite like this.

He leaned against the counter, wineglass in hand. 'Will you miss me, Lesley?'

'Just the same way I miss a toothache when it stops hurting.'

He considered her reply, and dismissed it. 'You could still come with me.'

'Why would I want to?'

'For the fun.'

'I thought you wanted me to stay at the *Woman* to smooth the transition?'

He shrugged. 'You wouldn't have to be here all of the time. And when you are, I could come with you.'

'Let's make it plain, Cade. I'm not interested in working for you, and I'm even less interested in living with you. All right?'

He ran an idle finger along the wood grain of a cabinet door. 'So you're going to marry Jay and live happily ever after?'

'I intend to marry him, yes.'

'I'll give twenty-to-one odds that you won't.' He sampled a mushroom. 'Hey, these are good.'

'It wouldn't be a fair bet. Your ego would be bruised again, Cade.'

'If you actually do marry him, it won't be because you prefer him. 'You'll do it because you're afraid of taking the risk of living with me.'

'That attitude does cover all angles. I was wrong—obviously your ego is unbruisable.' She finished the mushrooms, spreading them out to drain and cool, and started on the cauliflower.

'You like playing it safe, don't you, Lesley? You're hiding from a relationship you want because you're afraid to find out what it could be like.'

'I remember what it was like last time, and that was plenty for me.'

'Nothing comes with a guarantee, my dear. Even your beloved Jay failed at marriage once. What makes you think this time will be better?'

She didn't reply. Whatever she said, he would have an answer; there was no way to explain to him why she cared so much for Jay. Cade was incapable of understanding love, she thought. She took the pan of golden brown rolls out of the oven.

'If we aren't going out for dinner . . .' he began.

'Don't let me stop you.'

'Are you going to feed me? I hate to see all this marvellous food go to waste.' He was eyeing the rolls as he spoke.

'I'll save it for tomorrow. Go home, Cade.'

'And leave you all alone? How thoughtless of me. Unless, of course, you have plans.'

'As a matter of fact, I do.' She met the challenging gleam in his eyes and lied, 'There's a movie on TV that I've been dying to see.'

The gleam turned into a humorous twinkle. 'In that case, I'll stick around and watch it with you. Hotel rooms are so boring.'

She should have expected that, Lesley told herself. 'Hand me the steaks,' she said. She might as well stop arguing; she'd end up feeding him anyway.

'I would never have suspected it,' Cade said during a commercial break halfway through the movie. 'You just don't seem the type to like horror films.' He looked up at her, eyes narrowed, from the floor; he was comfortably sprawled on the carpet at her feet.

Lesley, curled up in an afghan rug on the couch, was feeling a little green from the first half. During one of the gory parts she'd had to pull the afghan over her head.

'Nice little place,' Cade murmured, looking up at the balcony rail. 'Is Jay going to move in here?'

'I suppose so.'

'Where are you going to put the nursery?'

'We aren't planning to have children.'

He looked her over thoughtfully. 'His decision, or yours?'

'It was mutual.' The movie came back on, and she

turned her attention to the screen. Horror film or not, it was better than the conversation.

A few minutes later, he said, 'What would you have named our child, Lesley?'

'Remember, Cade? There was no child.'

'Thornton still thinks there was.'

'Mr Thornton is an egotistical maniac who can't bear to think he might be wrong. You two have a lot in common, you know.'

He rearranged his pillow into a more comfortable shape and said idly, 'Why don't you want Jay's children, Lesley?'

'It has nothing to do with Jay. I just don't think I can have a job and be a mother, and I don't want to quit working.' She tossed the afghan aside. 'Do you want another glass of wine?'

He handed her the stemmed glass without comment.

In the kitchen, out of his sight for a few moments, she leaned against the refrigerator and took several deep breaths. 'Please hurry, Jay,' she thought. But she supposed Cade had planned that, too, and ordered Mr Thornton to keep Jay occupied.

Damn Mr Thornton anyway, she thought. Cade had seemed willing to let the past drop. If only that damned attorney would do the same!

She set her own wineglass on the coffee table and bent over Cade to give him his. But his eyes were closed, his breathing deep and regular. She sighed. That was all she needed, to have Jay walk in to find a sleeping Cade on her floor.

She put his glass next to hers so he could reach it, and uttered a little scream as his hand closed suddenly around her wrist. 'I thought you were asleep,' she accused.

'Obviously you were wrong.' He tugged gently on her wrist, pulling her down on the carpet beside him. 'I was just daydreaming of you.'

'Cade, I'd rather watch the movie.' She was breathless.

'Liar.' The word was totally without heat. 'You hated every minute of it.'

'Not as much as I dislike this,' she countered.

His eyes sparkled. 'Prove it.' His fingers gently found her breast under the sweater, and a long shiver ran through Lesley. He kissed her throat, nibbling his way up the slender column, stroking the sensitive patch under her ear, running his fingers through her hair. His whole body was like fire pressed against hers, and Lesley felt the stirring of passion coming to life deep within her.

Her conscience tingled. This was something far too dangerous to play with. 'Stop,' she murmured. 'Oh, please stop.'

'Can he do this to you?' Cade said against her lips. 'If he can make you feel this way, Lesley, then I'll stop. I'll go away.' He pulled back for an instant to look at her, then with a groan he crushed her mouth under his. The kiss was like an explosion tearing through her, ripping away the frail façade behind which Lesley had hidden for so long, freeing the fire of passion that she had kept banked down for so many years.

'Look at me, Lesley,' he demanded. 'Open your eyes.'

'Why?' she breathed, but she obeyed.

'I want to see what colour they are now. And I want there to be no doubt about who is making love to you. I don't want you to pretend that I'm Jay.'

'Who's pretending?' It was an effort to speak, so she put her hands on the back of his neck, silently tugging him down to her again.

His mouth was teasing and demanding by turns, and soon Lesley was making demands of her own. A button from his shirt went spinning across the carpet, and Cade lifted his head. 'Impatient, my darling?'

He pulled away from her and Lesley murmured a protest. He smiled and tugged her sweater over her head, tossing it aside, then turned his attention to the lacy bra. When it was disposed of, he bent his head to her breast, caressing the delicate tip with his lips.

His hand wandered over smooth ivory skin to the fastener of her jeans, then under the denim to caress the softness of her stomach and the curve of her hip. Lesley wriggled under his touch as shivers darted through her. She wrapped herself around him and tried to pull him down to her, but Cade was determined to take his time.

The doorbell chimed, the four opening notes of Beethoven's Fifth sounding harsh and strident.

Lesley's eyes flew open in horror. 'Jay!' she breathed.

'I guess. Is his timing always this bad?' Cade sighed. 'It should be interesting to see his face when he uses his key.'

She struggled in his arms. 'He doesn't have a key.'

'Then perhaps we should let him in. Now is as good a time to tell him as any, I suppose.'

'Tell him—what?' Lesley said. She stopped struggling for a moment.

'That you're not going to be seeing him any more, dummy.' He dropped a gentle kiss on her lips. 'Because you're going to be too occupied with me.'

Lesley was unresponsive. 'I never said I was going anywhere with you. And if you think I'm going to stand here and break my engagement because of a kiss, you're crazy.'

His eyes narrowed. 'Pretty exotic kissing, Lesley. And if Jay had been five minutes later, there wouldn't be any explaining to do. He'd be able to see it all for himself.' He released her and reluctantly stood up.

She wasn't listening. 'Hurry, Cade. You'll have to go out the back door——'

He tucked his shirt in. 'When are you going to stop fooling yourself, Lesley? You say you want the freedom that men have. The freedom of the bedroom, you called it. All right, you've got it. Now are you going to use it or are you going to wonder for the rest of your life what would have happened if you had slept with me?'

'Just get out of here!' she demanded in a harsh whisper.

'Lesley?' Jay called. 'Are you all right?'

'I'm coming!' she said. 'I was . . . in the shower. Be there in a minute.' She fastened her bra and reached for her sweater.

Cade got to it first. She tried to pull it out of his hands, but he held on. 'Can Jay set that soft skin of yours on fire?' he asked, tracing the outline of her bra with a gentle fingertip. 'I'll bet he's never even seen what I'm looking at now. Are you satisfied with that, Lesley? Is that passionless, spineless creature what you want in your bed?'

'All I want is for you to leave me alone,' she said fiercely.

'You've got it. But I warn you, my dear. There is some kind of magnetism between us, and saying it isn't there won't make it disappear. You want me as badly as I want you, and whether you live with me or not, I will always be a ghost in your bed. You might sleep with Jay, but it will be my name you call out when he makes love to you.' He picked up his jacket and thrust her sweater into her hands.

She heard the kitchen door click shut behind him as she zipped the sweater with shaking fingers. She took a deep breath, smoothed her hair, and let Jay in.

'What took you so long?'

'I told you. I was in the shower. Did you reach an agreement?'

Jay shrugged. 'Perhaps. It still has to get Cade's approval tomorrow, but Mr Thornton seems to think he'll like it. Have you had company?'

Lesley, following his glance, spotted the two full wineglasses on the coffee table. 'Oh—no,' she improvised. 'I forgot I'd left one in here, and then I poured myself another one.'

Jay looked a little confused. 'That doesn't sound like you.'

'I'm just tired, Jay.'

'I won't stay long.' He walked over to the couch, then stooped to pick up a small, gleaming object at his feet. 'You lost a button, Angel.'

Lesley gulped and took it out of his hand before he had a chance to examine it. 'It must be from my new white blouse. They don't sew them on very well any more.' She knew she was babbling, but she didn't seem to be able to stop.

Jay didn't seem to notice. He sat down with a heavy sigh and ran his hands through his hair.

'I'm so tired I can't even be angry at you, Angel.'

She curled up in a chair and studied him. Jay looked exhausted, his three-piece grey suit rumpled and his tie loose. Jay, who never appeared anywhere without a fresh crease in his trousers and a new, tight knot in his tie.

'About the cake . . .' she said, and hesitated. Her mind was beginning to spin from all the whoppers she was telling. It was becoming difficult to keep her stories straight.

'Don't bother to explain. I don't think I could stay awake through the whole story. It didn't seem to matter, anyway, because the negotiations went on just as usual. I wouldn't have been surprised if the stunt with the cake had upset Cade so much that he'd have broken off the deal, Lesley.'

'I am sorry, Jay.'

'And of course Mother was livid. She doesn't understand why you can't act like a lady. And frankly, Angel, neither do I. I've never before seen behaviour like that from you.'

You've never before seen me with Cade Randall needling me, Jay, she thought.

'You have some fences to mend with Mother. She told me last night that she refused to have anything to do with you any more. No wedding reception, no nothing. You'll have to work her around again.' He rumpled his hair again. 'Though it will make it easier to postpone our wedding, this way, so you can work a few more months.'

'Is that clause still in the contract?' Lesley asked quietly.

Of course. Randall's no fool.'

She came across the room to him, impulsively kneeling at his feet, her hands in his. 'Jay, let's go away. Let's leave it all and move somewhere else. Just the two of us. Think about it! No more quarrels with your mother, and . . .'

'My mother is looking out for my best interest, Lesley.' Jay's voice was stiff.

'And no more problems with Cade Randall . . .'

'Are you suggesting again that I not sell the magazine? We've been through all that, Angel.'

She shook her head. 'No. I understand that you have to sell it now. But we don't have to stay in Chicago, Jay. I'll freelance. I can do that anywhere.'

'You'll be under contract to Cade for at least six months, Angel. You can't run out on that.'

'Why can't I?' she demanded. 'I haven't signed anything, or made any agreement to work for him. And you can't sell him my contract because I don't have one. He can't hold me to anything you sign, Jay.'

'I've made a gentleman's agreement.'

'That term presupposes that there are two gentlemen making the deal—and that certainly isn't the case here,' she said tartly.

'You gave me your word, Lesley. And I gave it to Mr Thornton. I told him that if Cade buys the magazine, you'll sign a contract.'

'Well, what if I change my mind? What can he do, sue me?' He wouldn't, a little voice in the back of her mind said. But he could make life awfully unpleasant.

They sat there in silence for a little while, and then Jay got up. 'I'd better go home,' he said heavily, 'or she'll be wondering where I am. I'll call you for lunch tomorrow if I'm free.'

Lesley shook her head. 'Tomorrow is deadline. No lunch.'

'All right.' He put a gentle kiss on her cheek.

Lesley clung to him, suddenly feeling that he was the only rock she could hang on to in a whole lakeful of waves. 'Jay? Kiss me. Really kiss me.'

He looked surprised, Lesley wrapped her arms around his neck, pulling him down till he met her lips. She kissed him eagerly, hungrily, willing herself to feel in the pit of her stomach the aching fire that had blazed when Cade kissed her. But there was no fire.

Jay pulled back. 'Lesley,' he said, sounding shocked. 'What's happened to you? There will be plenty of time for that when we're married.'

'Why should we wait?' she asked fiercely. 'We're adults. Sexual feelings don't just turn on automatically when the marriage licence is signed, you know.'

'But waiting makes the experience far more precious. I don't expect you to understand, Angel. You're inexperienced, I know it's hard for you to wait, but believe me, it's worth it.'

She wanted to throw her arms around him and beg. Take me to bed, Jay, she wanted to say. Make love to me, make me forget Cade Randall. Because unless I feel that I really belong to you, in every way, I may not be able to hold out. I'm a woman, Jay, and I have needs. If you don't meet them, he will.

But of course she couldn't say it. Tears pooled in her eyes.

'When we're married, Angel, you'll see that I'm right.' He brushed a tear off her long lashes. 'Oh, my Angel, it isn't that I'm rejecting you. It's just that you deserve much more than some hurried, sordid little encounter when we're both tired and overworked. There's a lifetime for that, darling.'

It isn't sordid, she wanted to say, not when two people care for each other. But Jay kissed her gently and pulled the door shut behind him.

She stared at the door. Then she lifted her clenched hand and opened it, staring at the deep imprint of Cade's button on her palm.

She went straight to her bedroom, seeking oblivion in sleep. But the silky pyjamas felt constricting, and rest eluded her. Whenever she closed her eyes, it was Cade she saw, his face hard as he had said, 'I will always be a ghost in your bed.'

Damn Cade Randall, she thought fiercely, punching her pillow and wishing it was him. Why did he have to come back into her life, upset everything just as she had succeeded in forgetting him and building a new relationship?

But had she forgotten him at all? Or had she fallen in love with Jay simply because he was Cade's opposite— because she didn't find Jay threatening?

She pushed back the blankets and walked restlessly through the condo. She didn't know where to look for her answer, but the question scared her.

She knelt on the carpet where he had so nearly made love to her, and found her fingers caressing the pillow he had used. It still carried a trace of his aftershave.

'Oh, don't be ridiculous, Lesley,' she told herself fiercely, and flung the pillow on to the couch. 'Stop mooning over the man like a lovestruck teenager . . .'

Lovestruck?

No. Never that. Cade was a remnant of her past, a loose end that she had avoided all these years. Now she needed to knot that loose end before her whole life unravelled.

She picked up the two delicate wineglasses and carried them to the kitchen. It wasn't until she had rinsed and dried them, careful of the fragile crystal, that she saw the slip of paper on the counter.

It was Cade's business card. Simple, stark, brown ink on buff-coloured pasteboard. Just his name and *Monsieur*'s trademark symbol. She turned it over. 'I'll wait for you,' he had scrawled on the back. Below it was a suite number.

'Damned sure of himself,' she muttered. But it was without heat.

He was a ghost. That was all. But unless she exorcised that ghost, Lesley knew, there would be no peace for her. He was right; she would always wonder, no matter what kind of man was in her life, whether she had chosen him because she was still running from Cade.

She stared at the card in her shaking hands. Then she put it down and went up to her bedroom to get dressed.

CHAPTER TEN

SHE almost lost her nerve in the hotel lobby. It was nearly deserted, and the porter seemed to be looking at her with a knowing smile. But she ducked her head into the collar of her woolly jacket and walked past him to the elevators.

Cade's suite had its own doorbell. She pressed it with trembling fingers.

It seemed forever before it was answered. She was almost ready to walk away when the door swung silently open.

Cade looked even taller and more forbidding on his own territory, she thought miserably. He was absolutely silent as she stood there, blocking the doorway, looking at her, a glass of wine in one hand, the other braced on the door.

She held out her hand. 'I brought your button back,' she said finally. If he makes a smart remark, she thought, I'll cry.

But he merely moved aside, gesturing for her to come in, Lesley stood there for an instant, staring up at him. Then she took the wineglass out of his hand, drained it in a gulp, and stepped across the threshold.

He closed the door behind her, and she heard the lock turn with a firm little click.

'Don't forget the chain,' she said without thought, and blushed beet-red.

'You're not seventeen anymore, Lesley,' he said gently. 'No one is going to intrude.'

She looked around the living room. His jacket lay across the back of a chair. On one of the couches papers spilled out of a manila folder. The telephone was on the coffee table, its cord stretching across the floor. Beside it was a half-full glass of wine.

Lesley looked down at the glass in her hand. 'You have a guest,' she said, feeling incredibly stupid. How did she always manage to get herself into situations like this, she wondered. Then fury rose in her. It was just like Cade, she thought; if he didn't succeed with Lesley, he had a second choice waiting in the wings.

He shook his head. 'That glass you're holding was waiting for you. It had got a little warm, I'm afraid. Would you like a refill?'

She looked at it curiously as he took it out of her hand, his fingers warm against hers. 'Were you so certain I would come?'

'To tell you the truth—I was beginning to think I was a damn fool, Lesley.' He didn't look at her; the subdued light threw angular shadows across his face as he poured the wine. His voice held no hint of humour, and there was—could she be mistaken?—uncertainty in his eyes as he held out the glass. 'I even told myself you might end up in bed with Jay tonight.'

So the great Cade Randall isn't always sure of himself after all, she thought. She shrugged out of her jacket and draped it over his on the back of the velvet chair. Then she took the glass out of his hand and set it on the table. Slowly she walked towards him until there was only the space of a breath between them.

'Do you know what you're doing, Lesley?' he asked.

'I need to find out some things about myself,' she said softly. She pulled his head down till his lips met hers in a fiery kiss that seemed to go on forever. His hands on the small of her back pressed her tightly against him, the whole length of her body moulded to him. When his hold loosened a bit, she ran slim fingers down the front of his shirt, caressing the spot where the button was missing. She didn't look up at him; she was suddenly shy of meeting the look in those dark eyes.

He released her abruptly and picked up his wineglass, staring at her moodily over the rim.

'Cade?' She was honestly confused, her senses still spinning from his kiss. She held out a hand to him, begging.

'Hell.' He set the glass down so hard that wine slopped over the rim. 'I ought to be wondering why you changed your mind, Lesley. But I don't give a damn as long as you are here.' He took her hand. 'Come with me.'

She went without hesitation. She had gone too far now to turn back.

The bedroom was even more elegant than the living room. The headboard of the kingsize bed was covered with pleated satin. The blankets were already turned down, and the lamps on either side of the bed glowed.

Lesley stood in the centre of the deep plush carpet and looked around for a moment. Cade didn't touch her, but she could see the hunger in his face.

She pulled her sweater slowly over her head and folded it neatly, kicked off her shoes, stepped out of her jeans. Cade still had not moved. She went to him, turning her back so he could unfasten her bra.

'My God, you're beautiful, Lesley,' he said, and his voice was almost hoarse.

When she was naked, her skin gleaming ivory in the dim light, she pushed the blankets back, lay down, and held out a hand to to to him.

He came to her slowly, as though he was reluctant to believe what he saw. He traced the course of a lock of dark hair as it spilled across the pillow, and said, 'Am I being seduced, Lesley?'

'I don't seem to be having much luck,' she murmured.

He laughed. 'You have no idea how successful you are.' His voice was husky.

She watched him undress, remembering the muscles rippling through his body, the lean physique without an extra ounce of flesh, the triangular mat of dark hair curling on his chest, with nostalgia that was almost painful.

When he came back to the bed, she reached eagerly for him, her fingernails teasing a gentle path down his back as she pulled him close.

'Watch those claws,' he warned, pulling her hand away. He kissed her palm, then turned her hand over and saw Jay's diamond gleaming on her finger. For a moment they were both still; he stared at her with a question in his eyes, then without a word he gently pulled the ring off and put it into her hand, folding her fingers gently over it.

Lesley looked up at him and then at the ring, set it on the bedside table, and reached for the switch on the lamp.

Cade stopped her. 'Leave the lights on,' he commanded. 'I don't want you to forget who is here in this bed with you.'

'You're unforgettable, Cade,' she said, and it was both an admission and a promise.

Their first caresses were tentative as they retraced the path of that night so long ago. But their hunger for each other soon banished all hesitation in the storm that carried them to peaks Lesley had never dreamed existed. And it was his name that she cried out in that final, ecstatic moment.

It seemed to her to be hours later that they lay, still tangled together, drifting back from the heights of their passion. Cade brushed a damp ringlet of hair back from Lesley's forehead with a gentle finger.

'Thank you,' she murmured huskily.

'Isn't that supposed to be my line?' Then, after a minute, he added gently, 'It's been a long time for you, hasn't it?' It wasn't really a question.

She nodded. It seemed to take all the strength she had left. She felt as if all her muscles had melted, leaving her paralysed. It took conscious effort to raise her hand to his cheek to caress the slight stubble of his beard.

He kissed her gently, nibbled her earlobe, brushed her love-swollen breast with his lips. But there was no passion left in him, either, and he gently pulled away from her.

She was reluctant to let him go, but she had no

strength left to hold him. He poked around in the drawer of the bedside table and held up a foil-wrapped block. 'Want a snack?' he asked.

She looked puzzled.

'Italian chocolate,' he explained, and broke off a piece. 'I had to substitute something when I quit smoking, and this is a quick energy restorer.'

'If you say so.' She obediently opened her mouth, and he put the square on her tongue.

'Looks as if you could use some energy,' he teased. He picked up her hand and let it drop, nerveless, back on to the blanket. 'You're so relaxed I'll bet you don't even have reflexes.' Then, suddenly, he turned serious. 'I will probably regret asking the question, but—Lesley, what are you going to tell Jay?'

She swallowed the chocolate and said, indistinctly, 'That you raped me.'

'I don't think he'll buy it.' Cade raised up on one elbow, leaned over her, and threatened, 'Especially after I confide to him everything that you whispered in my ear while we were making love.'

Lesley closed her eyes and sighed. 'It's not very gentlemanly of you to kiss and tell.'

'Neither is rape, but I have to admit that you have tempted me sometimes. You're tempting me right now, in fact.'

She looked up at him, startled. 'All I'm doing is lying here . . .'

'Looking so damned beautiful, with your eyes still that steamy grey and my kisses still on your lips . . .' He rolled over on his back, pulling her along so that she was sprawled full-length on top of him. 'I want you, Lesley.'

She whispered, 'And I want you, Cade . . .'

Sunshine was streaming in the windows when she woke, pouring across the carpet in pools. Lesley flung out a hand to the other side of the bed, but Cade wasn't there. There was, however, a single dark-red rose, its petals half open, lying on his pillow.

She buried her nose in the velvet petals, thinking about what a romantic he was after all, underneath that slick surface. Then she realised how high the sun was. And today was deadline—of all days to show up late at the office, she thought, she had to choose the most noticeable one.

The taxi ride seemed unbearably slow; Lesley thought she could have walked almost as quickly. She checked her watch, nibbled on her thumbnail, looked at the watch again. She hadn't overslept so badly in a year. Of course, she had to admit, there had been good reason—but that wasn't going to make it any easier to explain to Shelah.

When the elevator passed the floor the magazine offices were on without stopping, she breathed a sigh of relief. That was what she had been most afraid of—running into some of her staff before she could exchange her jeans for her usual Monday-morning attire. Not that it was any of their business what she chose to do on Sunday nights—but Lesley would rather talk to Jay herself, before the rumours started.

Oh, God—what am I going to tell Jay? she asked herself as she hurried down the hall to her condo. You had to go and complicate things, Lesley.

Shelah, waiting at the door of the condo, looked up at her approach and took her finger off the doorbell. She looked Lesley over without hurry, focusing on her rumpled hair and the rose in her hand.

'It's fortunate for all of us that you showed up,' she said finally. 'I was just about to call the building superintendent and get the pass-key so I could discover your murdered body.'

'I was . . . out.'

'Obviously,' Shelah said drily. 'You didn't answer the phone or the door, and Jay . . .'

'My God! You didn't call Jay, did you?'

'It was my next assumption.' Shelah sounded defensive. She followed Lesley into the condo. 'But it didn't seem to fit your pattern, so I was going to call the super instead. Where have you been, anyway, if you haven't been with Jay?'

Lesley started up the spiral steps. 'I'm going to take a shower and brush my teeth. Be a good assistant and go away, will you, Shelah?'

'Don't you know that a smart girl carries a toothbrush in her handbag at all times?' Shelah called up the stairs. 'Roses are romantic, but he'd never think of sending you a toothbrush tied up with a red ribbon.'

Lesley leaned over the balcony rail. 'And just what makes you think there was a man involved?'

'I've been looking for you for two hours, Lesley. You certainly didn't just run downstairs to pick up a quart of milk for breakfast. Or even because you had a sudden longing to smell a red rose.' She looked at her watch. 'I'm going back to work. If you're not there in half an hour, I'm coming up again to be sure you didn't fall asleep.'

'I'll be down in fifteen minutes.'

'Promises, promises,' Shelah muttered and slammed the door behind her.

But it was very close to a quarter of an hour later that Lesley came in. Her hair was loose; three minutes with a curling brush had turned it into a tangle of curls that looked as if she had planned it. Her dress was dark red, narrow-waisted and long sleeved, with a flared skirt. Her make-up was perfect.

And if I ever get a chance to catch up on my breathing, I'll be fine, Lesley told herself.

Shelah was at the drawing board in Lesley's office. 'I told everyone you were sleeping off a hangover,' she said without looking up.

'Gee, thanks,' Lesley muttered.

'Actually, the issue is under control. We only needed you because you're frying the chicken this afternoon for the recipe contest party.'

'Why do I always get the fun jobs? That picture would be much more effective if you'd run it bigger, Shelah. Crop it a little tighter.' She reached for two strips of white paper and laid them across the unnecessary parts of the photograph.

Shelah reached for her eraser. 'Why do you always have to be right? It's a very aggravating habit.'

Lesley wasn't listening. She was looking across the main office, watching the florist's delivery man as he came straight towards her office.

It didn't require any intuition to know what was under that tissue paper, Lesley thought. She watched as her secretary signed the receipt and brought the flowers to her door.

Jana looked intrigued. Flowers three times in the last week, her eyes were saying as she wordlessly set the vase on Lesley's desk.

Shelah waited till the door closed behind the secretary before she turned around on her stool to watch Lesley remove the tissue paper. Twelve enormous dark-red roses peeked out at her, so large that they looked too heavy to be supported by the slender stems.

'No wonder you overslept,' Shelah said dryly. 'It must have been some night.'

Lesley slit open the tiny envelope. It was unlike Cade to send a card, she thought. Jay might see it. But then, she supposed, the thought of Jay wasn't bothering Cade much today. She smiled just a little, thinking about him.

Then the smile froze as the contents of the envelope tumbled into her hand. Four small pieces of paper, edges roughly torn. One fluttered to the floor, and Lesley's signature, in bright green ink, stared up at her from the carpet. She stooped to pick it up with trembling fingers. It was the cheque she had given Cade, torn into quarters, returned to her in a sealed envelope without another word.

Like any other streetwalker, she had been paid for her favours, Lesley thought bitterly. She supposed that she should be flattered at the price he had put on their night together. But it didn't make her feel any less like a prostitute. She felt dirty suddenly, unbearably cheap. It hadn't been magic after all, last night; it had been strictly business to Cade.

She put the pieces of the cheque back into the tiny envelope, ignoring Shelah's curious gaze, put the envelope in her briefcase, and snapped the lock shut. 'I'm going to get a cup of coffee,' she announced in a voice that trembled only slightly.

In Colombia, she nearly added. Or somwhere that Cade Randall will never find me again.

Her coffee poured, she wandered through the offices. The minutes were ticking towards deadline; normally she would be poring over last-minute changes, those tiny improvements that made the difference between a good issue and an outstanding one. But today it didn't seem to matter.

Her advertising manager waved her over, and she sat down on the corner of the woman's desk. 'Lesley, I think I've had a brainstorm. How would you like to offer a needlework kit with each new subscription? That would bring in a lot of gift-givers. Or . . .'

Lesley's eyes were drawn as if by a magnet to the receptionist's desk. Cade stood there, looking across the room towards her office. Then he glanced around and came towards her.

Lesley's heart started to pound. She slid off the desk, ignoring the advertising manager's question, and started for her office. She was not going to have a scene with Cade Randall while twenty of her employees looked on.

He caught up with her short of the door. 'Good morning.' His voice was gentle, and his eyes caressed her as intimately as his hands ever had. 'You forgot to pick this up, Lesley. You'll want to return it to Jay.' He took her hand, dropping the diamond ring into it.

Lesley shivered as if he had kissed her. 'Now why would I do that, Cade?' she asked coolly. She didn't look at him.

He laughed. 'You can't mean that you're going to keep it?'

'Not only keep it. I plan to wear it.' She glanced up at him, intending to fix him with a challenging stare. But the fire in those big brown eyes made her look down at the carpet instead.

'Why, Lesley?'

'I don't care to discuss it here.'

There was an instant of silence. 'Then let's go somewhere else.' He reached for her arm.

Lesley pulled away. 'In fact,' she parried, 'I'm not certain that I care to talk about it at all. It really is none of your business, after all.'

'The hell it isn't,' he said. His voice was quiet, but it was icy.

'Lesley!' The cheerful cry came from across the office.

She turned, grateful for the interruption, and saw Bob Merrill coming across the office at breakneck pace.

The agent dodged between desks, waving a fat manila envelope over his head. 'Lesley, darling, it's dynamite! I had no idea things like that ever happened to you.'

'Things like what?' she asked faintly.

'The book, my dear. The book! I've never had a manuscript that was so easy to sell in my hands before. It's going to be a best-seller, you know.' He patted the envelope paternally.

'What do you mean, easy to sell, Bob?' Horror crept into her voice. 'I told you I'm not finished with it . . .'

He waved the objection away. 'Of course not. It needs rewriting; they always do. But I got fifty thousand in advance for you, with another two hundred thousand as soon as the manuscript is finished. How do you like that, Les—a quarter of a million dollars before they sell a copy. That's what I mean, dynamite!'

Cade's eyes had narrowed. 'What is this magnificent work about, Lesley?'

She looked up at him. 'Why—do you think it might have something to do with you?'

'It crossed my mind.'

'What an egotistical thought, Cade. You have nothing to worry about.'

'Maybe the *Woman* would like to buy the serial rights, Les,' Bob speculated, 'I think I'll give Jay a call. It might be just the thing to make him get into the book market.'

'Jay doesn't own the *Woman* any more,' Cade's voice was quiet, but absolutely authoritative.

Lesley wheeled around. 'You bought it?'

'We signed the papers a few minutes ago, I came straight here to tell you—to ask you to celebrate with me.' He raised an eyebrow questioningly. 'It's surely no surprise to you, Lesley.'

She stared at him, remembering that he had asked her once what it was worth to her for him to buy the magazine, implying that if she slept with him, he would make the purchase. The sudden realisation of what had happened hit her like a blow in the stomach. When she had gone to him last night, he thought she was answering his question. He thought that was why she had slept with him.

Her voice was low and firm. 'Go stick your celebration in your ear, Cade.' She turned her back on him. 'Bob, what if I don't want to sell it after all? I never dreamed—I only gave it to you to read and criticise . . .'

'What kind of fruitcake are you, Lesley? Sure, it's a little personal—maybe you want to use a pen name. But you can't condemn something as powerful as this to the dark. It needs to be said, and you're the only woman I know who can say it.'

She shook her head.

Bob sighed. 'I'll let you think about it. Let's have lunch tomorrow and talk it over.'

'It won't change my mind, Bob. I've had a chance to think about it, the last couple of days.'

'Well, if you decide to end the discussion by destroying the manuscript . . .'

'It's mine, Bob.' She held out her hand. 'You can't keep it when I want it back.'

'That's true.' He gave her the envelope reluctantly.

'But just in case you do something foolish—I kept a copy.' He looked thoughtful. 'I've protected manuscripts from tropical storrms, house fires, outraged lovers, and editors who leave them on commuter trains—but never before from the author.'

'If I don't want it published, that's my decision.'

'Lesley, keep it up and you'll be shopping for a strait-jacket. Mr Randall, if you want to publish some novels in your new magazine . . .' he put a business card into Cade's hand. 'I'd certainly appreciate the chance to talk about it.'

Cade pocketed the card thoughtfully, and Bob left, still muttering under his breath, Lesley was sure that she did sound crazy, to anyone who didn't know the circumstances. What in heaven's name had made her choose this week to take that manuscript to Bob? And why hadn't he taken the full two weeks he had asked for to read it? Then Cade might never have known about the book. In two weeks Cade would be back in New York . . .

Without her. It hit her suddenly with the weight of the world.

And that's exactly what I want, she told herself firmly. I want him to go away, and leave me alone, I never want to see him again.

She picked up the envelope and went into her office. Cade was right behind her.

Shelah looked up from the drawing board with a smile. 'Did the coffee calm you down?' she asked. 'Hi, Mr Randall.'

'Mr Randall has just bought the magazine, Shelah.' Lesley walked round her desk and sat down behind it.

Shelah didn't seem surprised. 'Welcome aboard,' she told him, and held out her hand. 'Or should that be the other way around?'

Cade laughed. 'Whichever it is, I'm glad that you approve, Miss Evans. Now, if you wouldn't mind—Lesley and I do have a few things to discuss.'

'Oh, of course. Why don't you stay around for the

recipe contest after the deadline? All the staff will be there. It's sort of our monthly reward for getting through all the work.'

'Thanks, I will. But we're not making an announcement till tomorrow—Jay and I are calling a press conference in the morning.'

'I'm sworn to silence.' Shelah scrambled her papers together. 'Don't forget you're frying the chicken, Lesley.'

'She seems to enjoy your office,' Cade said quietly after Shelah left. He closed the blinds that blocked out the rest of the offices, shutting them in together.

Lesley didn't argue. They might as well get it all over with right now.

'Would you like to tell me what you're angry about this morning?' he asked.

Lesley braced her hands on the edge of her desk. 'So you bought it,' she said. Her tone was light, conversational.

Cade looked wary. 'Yes, I thought you'd be pleased, since it does solve Jay's problem. One of them, at least.'

Her voice rose. 'And you seem to think that the deal you and Jay made included me—buy the magazine, get Lesley as—as some kind of bonus!'

'Lesley . . .'

She stumbled on, her eyes filling with tears. 'Well, Cade, your mistake was in not getting me to sign a contract before you made the purchase. Because whatever Jay agreed to, I refuse to have anything more to do with you.' She pulled the typewriter table over to her desk and rolled a sheet of *Today's Woman* letterhead into it. Three rapid sentences later, she yanked the paper out, scrawled her name at the bottom, and thrust it into his hand.

He had stood absolutely still in the centre of her office while she typed; he looked only mildly interested when she pushed the letter at him. 'You're resigning from the magazine?'

'Do I have to go up on the roof and scream "I quit"?'

He read the letter, folded it, put it in his breast pocket. His expression was noncommittal as he said, 'You could still come back to New York with me.'

Lesley laughed shakily. 'How much does it take, Cade? A brick wall falling on you?' She pulled the briefcase across the desk to her; her fingers fumbled with the combination lock. 'I found out what I wanted to know last night. And it's well worth the fifty thousand dollars to be rid of you, Cade.' Her voice cracked. The lock clicked open and she pulled out the pieces of the cheque. 'Now, will you leave me alone?' she said, and threw them at him.

He was angry then, his eyes full of icy fury that frightened Lesley. He gathered up the torn fragments of paper with an economy of motion that could not conceal the violence he wanted to express. He took the gold lighter from his pocket and set one of the fragments on fire, holding it till the flames touched his fingers.

Lesley cried, 'Stop it, Cade! You'll hurt yourself!'

He looked at her then. 'Perhaps that's what I want to do,' he said coldly. He dropped the fragment into an ashtray and reached for another.

She seized his arm, trying to keep him from repeating the action. But he shook her off, pushing her down into a chair, and set the remaining sections afire in the ashtray, stirring them dispassionately with a fingertip until the cheque was reduced to ashes.

'I'll write another one,' she threatened.

He brushed ashes off his hands, and said, his voice absolutely level, 'Try it, Lesley. Just try it. And then watch what I do to that one.' He stared at the vase of roses, his mouth twisted. 'I'm sorry to have inflicted the flowers on you. Obviously last night did not mean the same thing to both of us.' He picked the vase up and dropped it with a crash in the wastebasket. Then, without a backward look, he strode out of the office.

Lesley huddled in the chair until the sound of the door slamming died. 'Oh, my God,' she said then, and her voice sounded raw in the silence. 'Oh, my God— what have I done?'

CHAPTER ELEVEN

NEVER to see him again. That was what she had demanded, and it looked as if Cade was going to give her exactly that.

Never to feel the caress of his hands . . . never the taste of his kisses . . . 'He tried to buy me,' she said aloud. But the words rang emptily in her ears. What did it matter?

Shelah knew what she was talking about. She had said it more than once—'Someday you'll meet the right man, Lesley . . . If you loved him, you couldn't stand it if you weren't sleeping with him.'

Love? Lesley closed her eyes, and all she could see was Cade, standing there with his arms folded across his chest, as if reserving judgment.

She would admit to feeling desire—he was so damned handsome. And curiosity—she was puzzled by what quality it was in him that drew her so irresistibly. And even lust—he must number among the world's best lovers.

But love? Had she fallen in love with Cade Randall?

The intercom on her desk buzzed, and she stood up shakily to reach for it. 'Mr Nichols is calling, Lesley,' the receptionist told her. 'And Shelah asked me to remind you about the chicken.'

Damn Shelah and her chicken, Lesley thought. And damn Jay too. And damn Cade and the *Woman* and . . .

'Hi, Jay.' She tried to keep her voice steady. She looked down at her hand, at the bare finger where his ring had left an indentation. Then she picked up the gleaming band from the desk blotter where she had tossed it.

'Hello, darling. I suppose you know by now that we signed the agreement this morning?'

'Yes. Cade told me.'

'I'm satisfied with the results, Angel, but I'm exhausted by all of the stress. I think I'll just go home for some sleep. I thought about asking you to come to dinner tonight to celebrate . . .'

'I'd rather not, Jay. Not tonight.'

'Then I realised that Mother would not be happy if we went out, but I'm afraid she'd be even less happy if I brought you home—she hasn't forgotten about the cake yet.'

And damn Emily Nichols, too, Lesley added to her list. 'Tonight's the staff party, Jay. It will last till all hours, I'm afraid.'

'I'd almost forgotten. Besides, it just doesn't feel right to be there when I don't own the magazine any more. It's Cade's party now. You do understand, Angel?'

She turned the diamond ring and watched the light fracture inside the gems. Oh, yes, I understand, she thought. It doesn't feel right to go when I just resigned, either. If I'm no longer on the staff . . . 'Jay, I need to talk to you.'

She could almost see him nod. 'Well, if tonight's out—you'll be at the press conference tomorrow, won't you? It's at ten—perhaps we can talk after that. Oh, and would you make sure to have coffee and cookies and everything there? We'll have to use the main office. There will probably be a lot of people coming.'

'Jay——' She stopped herself with an effort. What difference did it make, whether she saw him today or tomorrow? If anything, by tomorrow she might know better what she wanted to say. Perhaps by tomorrow she wouldn't want to tell him anything at all, she thought. The whole business with Cade was behind her; by tomorrow she might be wearing Jay's ring again. 'I'll take care of the coffee,' she said quietly.

'I'll see you then, Angel. Have a good night's rest, now that all the confusion is over.'

Jay's confusion might be over, she thought drearily. But why do I feel that mine is only beginning?

* * *

Staff parties were always loud and long and enjoyable; the tension that built through the entire office in the few days before deadline dispersed with a bang at the party. But seldom were they quite as noisy as this one, Lesley thought, putting a hand to her aching head. Of course, Cade's presence accounted for part of it. Every feminine staff member wanted to impress him with her charm and reliability. It made Lesley tired just to watch them.

She fried what seemed like a ton of chicken, and all the time she was aware that across the room Shelah was flirting with Cade. And what did you expect, Lesley, she asked herself crossly. Shelah flirts with everybody. And Cade wouldn't wear his heart on his sleeve even if he had a heart.

But now and then she knew that he was watching her. She didn't have to look up, she could simply feel his gaze. And even though a room full of people separated them, she felt as if he was touching her each time he looked towards her.

The next time she felt the familiar tingle in the nape of her neck that told her he was watching, she turned to stare back at him, hoping to embarrass him into leaving her alone. But the expressionless look in those big brown eyes didn't waver, and it was Lesley's gaze that fell first.

Then the hot oil in the skillet popped and splattered over the back of her hand, and Lesley jerked away, shrinking from the sudden intense pain.

Cade had seen. He was beside her before anyone else was aware of what had happened, holding her hand under a stream of cold water. His arm was tight around her. He ran a gentle finger across the wet skin where the oil had made angry welts. 'Are you all right?'

'It's just a minor burn, Cade. It will stop hurting in a minute.'

'It wasn't just the burn that I was asking about.'

She raised her head, surprised. His voice was a little unsteady, and his eyes were intent on her face. She nodded slowly. 'I'll be fine, Cade.'

No, you won't, she told herself suddenly. Not if he goes away, Lesley. You won't ever be all right again. She stared up at him, and her eyes widened.

In that instant, she faced the truth. Despite the past, the misunderstandings, the hurt—despite everything, she had fallen in love with him. She wondered vaguely what would happen if she turned to him, put her arms around him, and begged for him to kiss her. But she didn't do it; she just stood very still and stared up at him.

His hand dropped slowly away from the small of her back, as if he were reluctant to let her go. Then he walked away.

Lesley watched him as he crossed the room, and she intercepted a thoughtful look on Shelah's face. Shelah didn't miss much, Lesley thought irritably. The quick brain beneath that fluffy blonde hair had no doubt already added up the score. She turned back to her chicken.

The evening dragged on, with taste-testing and voting and arguing about the merits of each recipe. It was late when the staff began to drift out. Most of them would recess to the cocktail lounge across the street, Lesley knew. Sometimes she joined them. Shelah almost always did.

She rinsed her coffee cup and put it in the dishwasher. There was no evidence left in the kitchen of the havoc that had reigned there just a few hours ago. Lesley looked around one last time and slipped away to her office.

She sat there in the dark, with only the light drifting through from the outer office, until everyone had gone. Shelah left with Cade; they were laughing as they went out.

Lesley's heart felt like a lump of ice. 'You had your chance,' she told herself. 'And you told him to get out of your life.' It didn't make it any easier, to hear the words.

She looked around, knowing that she should clear

her personal things out of the office tonight. But there were so many things—four years of her life had been spent in this little square room. Tomorrow would do well enough.

She opened the briefcase, picked up the fat envelope that Bob had brought her. She'd burn it, and tomorrow she would insist that Bob destroy the copy he'd made. It had been dumb of her to ever write it all down. To publish it would be insanity, pen name or not. No amount of money was enough to make her spread her lifeblood out for the casual reader.

She dropped the envelope into the case and snapped it shut. Then she looked around the office again, knowing that this was the last time she would see it this way. Tomorrow there would be reporters all over, recording the end of one era and the beginning of another. The staff would be in an uproar. A new editor would be anxious to move in.

Shelah, probably, she thought dispassionately. She was good. She deserved her chance. And if she got to the editor's desk by way of Cade Randall's bed . . . 'That's how Cade works,' Lesley told herself quietly. 'No one should expect him to change.' It wasn't Cade's fault if her needs were more than he could meet. Love had no place in Cade's vocabulary.

The scent of roses tickled her nose, and she dropped suddenly to her knees beside the wastebasket. The vase had shattered when Cade dropped it, but the roses peeked out over the rim of the basket, looking a little dejected.

'Leave them here,' Lesley ordered herself. 'Let the cleaning people take them home, or throw them out. It will only prolong the agony if you keep them.' But even while she was forming the words, her hands were busy, plucking the long stems out of the basket, untangling the foliage from the shattered glass, wrapping them carefully in the tissue paper that had covered them earlier. 'You're absolutely foolish, Lesley,' she condemned herself. But she knew that she would keep the roses alive as long as she could.

Everything seemed unreal as she left the office. It all looked as if it were a photograph taken with a slightly out-of-focus lens. She locked the plate-glass door for the last time—she must remember to turn in her key tomorrow, she reminded herself—and stepped into the elevator. 'I've spent the best part of my life in elevators,' she mused.

She'd have to talk to Jay, of course. It was impossible to marry him, now that she knew how she really felt about Cade. It would be difficult to make him understand.

Perhaps she would just sell the condo, too, she thought, leaning against the carpeted wall of the elevator and closing her eyes. There were always other condos and other places; Chicago wasn't the only city in the world, after all. Magazines were published everywhere. It would be easier to get a new start somewhere else.

The elevator announced her floor with a discreet chime, and she opened her eyes. She was almost to the condo before she saw Cade. He was leaning against the wall opposite her door, arms folded, waiting patiently.

It was hard to breathe. She faltered a little, her steps slowing. He just stood there quietly and watched her approach, and when she came to a halt a few feet from him, he said softly, 'You salvaged the roses.'

She looked down at the flowers, clutched in her hand, as if surprised that they were still there. 'They're so expensive.' Her voice was a bare whisper.

He shook his head slowly. 'That's not why you kept them, Lesley.'

'No.' The word was a mere breath.

He pushed himself away from the wall then and held out a hand for her key. He didn't demand it; it seemed that he was making a simple request for something that was rightfully his. She fumbled it out of her handbag.

He unlocked the door and dropped the key into the pocket of his jacket. Then he took her hand and led her gently, as he would have led a confused child, into the apartment.

He followed her to the kitchen. 'You left with Shelah,' she said as she ran water into a milk glass vase.

'I walked out to the elevator with her,' he corrected.

'Did she know you were coming up here?'

'Shelah doesn't miss much.' He watched her arrange the roses with hands that trembled a bit. 'Does it matter?'

'No.' She toyed with the flowers, exchanging two of them, pulling another forward so it showed off better, tugging at the foliage till it framed the heavy petals to perfection.

'Whenever you've finished playing with those,' Cade said gently, 'I'd like to have your full attention.'

She sighed and pushed the vase away. 'Do you want a cup of coffee or something?'

'Or something,' he said. He put his hands on her shoulders; the contact shivered through her like an electric current. 'I want to make love to you, Lesley.'

She swallowed hard and clenched her hands against the insane desire that flooded through her, the longing to fling herself into his arms and beg him to love her.

'Why?' she asked. 'Wasn't last night expensive enough for you?' She intended it to be sarcastic, but the question was only a whisper.

He frowned. 'What is that supposed to mean?'

'I know I should be flattered that you're willing to pay so much for me.' Her voice broke, and she looked down at her hands clasped on the edge of the kitchen counter. 'But I'm not,' she whispered. 'I am not a prostitute, Cade.'

He looked stunned. 'My God, Lesley, no one ever said you were.'

'But you did.' She looked up then, anger lighting her eyes. 'You paid me off—a fifty thousand dollar debt cancelled. I'm glad you enjoyed last night, Cade, but was it really worth that much to you?'

'Now that you mention it, it was worth far more,' he mused.

'And today you bought the magazine.'

'So what?' His voice was wary.

'I was the bait. If I slept with you, you'd buy it—make it easy for Jay. You told me that, remember? What did that one cost you, Cade? Fifteen million?'

'Twelve and a half. And a bargain it is, too.'

'What? Me?' Lesley snapped bitterly. She tried to push past him, but he blocked her way.

'No, spitfire. The magazine. It would have been worth the price if he'd asked twenty.' He pushed his jacket back and put his hands in his trouser pockets. 'Oh, hell, Lesley, of course I said that. I think I would have said anything that night if it might have made you think about what you were doing.'

'You thought I should reconsider turning down the great Cade Randall.'

'No. You were about to marry a man you didn't care about. You would have been miserable with Jay, and if you possess the smallest scrap of honesty you already know that, Lesley.' The fire in his eyes challenged her to argue with him. 'Do you really think I bought the magazine because you spent the night with me?'

It did sound a little out of reason. Lesley wouldn't look at him.

'I'd made up my mind to buy it last week.'

'You had?' she whispered.

'You don't think that sales contract was drawn up this morning, do you?'

'And the cheque?'

He sighed. 'If I had possessed ordinary common sense, I would have burned the damn thing in front of you last night, before you ever set foot in my bedroom. But to be frank, Lesley, I didn't expect you to do what you did last night, and I was off balance. You have that effect on me, my dear.'

'So why did you send it this morning?'

'Because I didn't want you to be in my bed only because you owed me money.' There was a long pause. 'Which was it, Lesley? Did you want to be there, or did I force you into it with the blackmail?' She was silent, and he sighed. 'Lesley, please tell me. Which was it?'

She stared at the gold chain that peeked out from the collar of his shirt. 'I wanted to be there,' she said finally.

He brushed the tangle of curls back from her cheek with a gentle finger. 'And has that changed?' he asked softly.

She raised her head slowly, and she knew that all her love and her longing showed in her eyes. 'No, Cade, it hasn't changed.'

He caught his breath, then his hands cupped her face gently, turning it up for his kiss.

Her mouth clung to his hungrily, her senses spinning. She stood on her toes, pressing her body against his, delighting in the firmness of his muscles under her hands.

How long? The question echoed in her mind. How long before the enchantment died, before he tired of her? Then she knew that she didn't care. Everyone lived on borrowed time, after all—marriages ended every day in divorce or unexpected death. Their situation would be no different, only plainer. And their time together would be even more precious for knowing that each day might be the last.

'Wouldn't you like to go change into something more comfortable?' Cade asked, his voice a bit unsteady.

'These shoes are killing me,' she agreed, and reluctantly left the warmth of his arms. 'I'll be back in a minute.'

At the top of the stairs, she hesitated, hearing a tuneless little whistle rising from downstairs. She smiled. Cade did care about her. That was all that mattered. A cork popped, loud in the quiet apartment.

She dropped her dress over the arm of a chair and kicked her shoes off on the closet floor. She reached for a floor-length caftan in a zebra stripe.

Cade climbed the stairs noiselessly and was beside her before she knew he was near. He set two glasses on the bedside table and took the caftan out of her hand. 'This might be comfortable for you—but it doesn't do much for me. Let me show you what I had in mind.' He traced the outline of the low-cut, lacy bra, and then removed it. The wispy nylon panties followed, and Cade said, standing back to look at her, 'Now that is an outfit I admire.' He reached for his wineglass.

'It feels a little strange to stand here like this when you're fully dressed,' Lesley pointed out.

'Fair is fair,' he agreed. 'In the meantime, I wouldn't want you to catch pneumonia ...' He turned the blankets back on the bed and deposited her in it, tucking her in with exaggerated care.

She propped herself up on one elbow.

'Satin sheets,' he mused, unbuttoning his shirt. 'Do you entertain often?'

She was irritated. 'That's none of your business.'

He raised an eyebrow. 'It isn't?'

'No. And besides, I happen to like the feel of satin against my skin.'

'That's what I thought.' He draped the shirt across the arm of a chair and sat down on the edge of the bed to take off his shoes and socks.

'Cade, your back!' She sat up suddenly, her irritation forgotten in concern for him. 'What happened? It's all scratched.'

'You should remember, my dear.'

'Did I do that?' she asked faintly.

'No,' he mocked. 'I ran into a leopard on Michigan Avenue and he wanted to say hello.' His trousers landed on the chair and he slid under the blankets beside her.

She snuggled into his arms. 'I'm sorry, Cade.'

'It's nothing. A few scars here and there—it's a small price to pay.' He nuzzled her throat. 'However, if it happens again, I'm going to trim your fingernails myself.'

'I'll be careful,' she promised.

His lips tugged gently at her earlobe, and his hand wandered down over her breast, tickling gently at her ribs, to the curve of her hip. 'Well, don't be too careful,' he said huskily. 'I rather like sleeping with a wildcat.'

The fire started to rise in her again, but she tried to fight it off. 'Cade—there are some things I should tell you.'

'Later.' He rolled over suddenly, pinning her to the bed. 'There will be all the time in the world to talk, later.'

It was a promise, and Lesley relaxed with a sigh and felt the flame of passion begin to rise once more.

The weight of an arm across her and the warmth of a body snuggled against her spine woke her. She extracted herself carefully from his embrace and watched him sleep for a while. He was frowning, as if concentrating on wringing the last few minutes of rest out of the night. Except that it wasn't night any more; the sun was shining weakly through the big windows that faced the lake.

Lesley looked at the clock and then pushed herself out of bed with an effort. If Cade was going to make it to his own press conference on time, she'd better start breakfast.

She came back a few minutes later with a cup of coffee and sat down on the edge of the bed. 'Cade?' she said.

He opened his eyes reluctantly. 'Why are you up in the middle of the night?' he asked indistinctly.

'It isn't. You have less than two hours to make it to a press conference.'

'Good. Wake me up again in ninety minutes.'

She waved the cup under his nose and he reluctantly sat up, propping the pillows against the headboard and taking the cup from her hands. 'You're a determined woman, Lesley Allen,' he informed her.

'Put your clothes on and I'll go fix breakfast.'

He studied her face, thoughtfully rubbing the back of his hand across his stubbly beard. 'I'd rather have breakfast in bed,' he said. In one swift movement he set the coffee cup aside and captured her, pulling her down on top of him.

'You're a sex maniac,' she murmured.

'I know. Nice hobby, isn't it?'

'Sex doesn't solve everything, Cade.'

'Of course not. But at least we'll never be without something to do.' He untied the belt of her terry robe. 'Or do you have a sudden aversion to making love to me?'

'The beard has seen better days,' she admitted.

'I'll shave just as soon as you cut the fingernails.'

'Did I do it again?'

'Yes. Not that I'm really complaining, mind you . . . But if you would like to salve the pain . . .' He patted her suggestively.

'Cade, it's absolutely crazy that I can't say no to you.'

'I think it's very nice,' he argued.

Their love play was slow and peaceful, without the heights of passion the night before had held, but with the beginning of easy familiarity. It was utterly satisfying, Lesley thought afterwards as they lay quiet in each others' arms, reluctant to let the outside world intrude.

But finally Cade sighed and pushed the blankets back. 'If I'm not going to look like a bum, I need a shower and a shave. And since I wasn't sure enough of myself last night to bring a suitcase——' He kissed her, long and warmly. 'I have to trek down to the hotel to change clothes.'

'Breakfast?'

'I just had the only kind I wanted.'

'Cade——'

'Yes, dear?'

She was going to say, I love you, but something stopped her, 'I'll see you at the press conference.'

After he left, she stayed in bed for a few minutes, then sat up and reached for the telephone. There was one very difficult piece of unfinished business yet before her. She still didn't know how she could explain it to Jay, but she couldn't wait any longer to try.

She had to talk to him before the press conference. If she didn't, Jay was certain to put his foot in his mouth by announcing their wedding date, or something even crazier.

The maid went to find Jay, leaving Lesley tapping her fingers nervously on the receiver. Then Emily picked up the telephone. 'Lesley,' she said firmly, 'I want you to stop this habit of yours of pestering Jay. He has a right to privacy, and I am tired of you interrupting our family.'

'Emily, dear,' Lesley said sweetly, 'when are you going to realise that Jay isn't twelve years old anymore? Perhaps he'd develop a little backbone, if you weren't sitting on his shoulder telling him what to do all the time.'

Emily's answer was to bang the telephone down on the table. Lesley jumped, but kept the phone to her ear. It was only a few moments later that Jay picked it up. She asked him mechanically to stop by the condo before he went to the press conference, and Jay, mechanically, agreed.

Then she got out of bed and put on one of her favourite autumn dresses, a deep green dress with lace on the collar and cuffs. It was a little more formal than she usually wore at the office, but this was a formal occasion.

When Jay rang the bell a little later, she greeted him with a coffee mug in her hand. She poured him a cup and led the way into the living room. Jay sat down stiffly.

Without comment, Lesley handed him the diamond ring. He looked at it closely, and then up at her. 'Are you returning this because of what you said to Mother this morning?'

'No. It's the reverse, actually—I said what I did because I was planning to return the ring. It won't work, Jay. I do love you, but I think I was looking for the father that I never had.'

He studied the ring, watching the light reflecting off the facets. 'What happened, Lesley?

She hesitated, thinking about it. 'In the last few weeks I've finally faced up to an important part of my life. You said last week that you thought I should write a book. It's funny that you said that—it's exactly what I've been doing. Remember that series of articles I wrote about parents who lose children? Crib death, all that sort of thing?'

'Vaguely.' Jay shrugged. 'I don't understand what you're getting at, Lesley.'

'As I talked to those people, Jay, I realised that they were facing their grief. I had tried to hide from mine. I had ignored for almost ten years the fact that my little girl was stillborn.'

The look on Jay's face might have been comical if it hadn't been tragic. 'You . . . had a baby?'

She hurried on. 'When I started to write about how I felt as the mother of a child who never took a breath—much less knew laughter or love—the walls began to break down.'

'You had an affair, Lesley?'

'Damn it, Jay, for once, will you just listen to me?'

Jay looked startled by her outburst, but he subsided.

'I felt betrayed when Melissa died. I loved her so. She would have belonged to me, as no other human being ever had. And I was afraid to love after that, Jay, for fear that I'd be hurt again.'

'Are you saying that you don't love me after all?'

'I do care about you. But it isn't in the way that I would want to love my husband.' Her voice was quiet.

'Lesley—it wouldn't matter if you had a dozen kids. It doesn't change how I feel about you.'

'Yes, it would, Jay. Because it's a good book. Last night I was ready to burn it. I was afraid to publish it because it was so personal, because someone might laugh at me for mourning so long and so badly. Today—well, Bob Merrill thinks he has sold it, and I think that I'll let him, because it might help someone out there. There are a lot of people who have lost children, and who are hurting the same way I did.'

'So you wrote a book. That's no big deal.'

'Your mother wouldn't like having my name on a book like that. For one thing, I wasn't married, you know.'

He hesitated, his internal war showing plain in his face.

'You wouldn't like it either, Jay. Be honest. If I went on a tour to promote a book like that——'

'Perhaps you're right, Lesley.' He laughed shakily, and said, 'Well, at least it isn't what I thought. I expected when you called me that your reason was Cade. I even suspected that you had been sleeping with him.'

Lesley stared at the bottom of her coffee cup, trying to find words to tell him. He would find out soon; there would be no secrecy. She must tell him the truth, or he would feel betrayed. He might even think she had lied about Melissa, and that would hurt. She didn't want to hurt Jay; he had been too good a friend.

'May I tell you about my daughter?' she asked quietly.

Jay made a weak gesture. 'Really, Lesley—I don't think . . .'

'I named her Melissa Ann,' she said. 'There isn't much to say about a baby who was born and who died. I don't even know what colour her eyes would have been. But her hair was black, and she was perfect.' She walked across the room, seeing instead the little hospital room where they had told her that her baby was dead. 'They never did really know why she died,' Lesley mused. 'Sometimes they never do with stillbirths. The babies are perfectly normal, but they die anyway.'

'Please, Lesley, I . . . don't think this is any of my business. It has nothing to do with us.'

Yes, it does, Jay, she wanted to say. It affects us because it is part of me—a very important part of me, a part I'm only beginning to accept. But Jay wasn't interested in hearing about that.

She looked at him for a long time, seeing a weak man, a man who had little interest in things outside himself—seeing a Jay she had never allowed herself to recognise before. 'You were right, you know,' she said finally.

He hesitated. 'About what?'

'About Cade. I've been . . . seeing him. I will go on seeing him.'

Jay's face tightened. 'Well. That does change things, doesn't it?'

She didn't answer.

Jay stood up decisively. 'He won't marry you, you know, Lesley.'

'It doesn't matter.' Her voice was quiet.

He paused at the door. 'How long do you think it will last? I must say, Lesley, I thought you had more sense.'

'Goodbye, Jay. I'll be down in a few minutes for the press conference.'

He didn't answer. She closed the door behind him with a sense of having burned her bridges. But that was all right too, she thought. At least she had finally seen Jay as he really was. She was glad to know it. If she had married him, the knowledge would have come as a dreadful blow.

It was his right to be shocked about Melissa, she concluded. She probably should have told him two years ago, before they had become involved. But then she had been trying to forget Melissa too, feeling that a ten-year-old sorrow should be allowed to die.

She'd almost done it, writing that dry, factual little book on stillbirth, feeling that she had risen above the pain, until an editor and an agent had pushed her into a more personal account. And until Cade had come back into her life to remind her of what she had suffered and given up.

She went back into the writing room. She'd get the manuscript out, and show it to Cade as soon as the press conference was over. And she would beg his forgiveness for the lies, and tell him the little there was to tell about his daughter.

But the briefcase wasn't where she was certain she had left it last night, in its usual place beside her desk.

She searched the room, and then the condo. Her manuscript was gone.

CHAPTER TWELVE

AND the only person who could have taken it was Cade.

Lesley sat down at her desk and stared at the walls, where bright green vines climbed over the shiny wallpaper. She mentally retraced her steps of the night before, frowning with the effort of remembering each event. She had looked at the manuscript down in her office, had put it back in the briefcase, had picked up the case . . .

Or had she? She'd been clutching her handbag and the roses last night, but had she carried the briefcase upstairs, or left it on her desk?

She nibbled on a fingernail, trying to remember. Then she decided the effort was pointless, so she dug her spare key to the condo out of her desk drawer and went down to the press conference.

Jay was already seated at the table that had been set up in the centre of the room, stiffly upright, arms folded on the flat surface. Cade was at the far end of the big office, already surrounded by reporters and staff members. His back was towards her, and Lesley didn't try to catch his attention; she went straight to her office.

But the briefcase wasn't there, either. She looked round carefully, trying to remember where she might have set it down. She asked Jana, who hadn't seen it. And she finally had to face the truth: the briefcase and the manuscript it had contained were nowhere to be found, and Cade was the only person with the opportunity, and probably the desire, to have removed it.

The press conference had started by the time she came out of her office. The main announcements had been made, and the reporters were pestering Cade for details on the new *Today's Woman*.

'And will Miss Allen stay on?' one of them asked. It was a giveaway question; he didn't even look interested.

Cade looked up at Lesley, leaning against the door of her office. He smiled at her and said. 'No. Miss Allen has other plans, and editing a magazine is not among them. She has resigned effective immediately.'

Lesley's hand closed tightly on the door frame; it was the only thing that kept her standing up. Vaguely she heard Cade continue, 'Shelah Evans will be the interim editor. She's been Miss Allen's assistant, and she'll take over till a permanent editor is named.'

Her head was spinning. How could Cade do this to her? she was screaming inside. Surely he knew how important her work was to her; she had certainly told him often enough. But the moment that she had tacitly agreed to live with him, he had set about eliminating everything else from her life—leaving himself as the only thing for her to concentrate on. Well, Cade Randall was going to get a surprise there.

The formal press conference over, the reporters milled around Cade and Jay, around Shelah, around Lesley.

'What are your plans, Miss Allen?' one asked.

'I'm looking at several possibilities,' she said woodenly. No sense in making a public quarrel out of it. The fact that murder was one of her options . . .

'Did you offer your resignation, Miss Allen, or were you asked for it?' another reporter demanded.

She looked at him with distaste. A couple of times they'd collided on stories, and Lesley had come out the winner. He probably hoped that she had been fired.

The answer came calmly from over her shoulder. 'Miss Allen offered her resignation. I accepted it reluctantly. She has no further comment.' Cade ushered her into her office, closed the reporters out, and shut the blinds.

He turned from the windows and swept her into his arms. 'Have I told you today how beautiful you are?' he asked, and kissed her.

It would have been a long, romantic kiss, but when Lesley remained absolutely unresponsive Cade sighed, let her go, and said, 'Oh, hell, Lesley. What did I do this time?'

She folded her arms defiantly and stared up at him. 'So you accepted my resignation reluctantly, hmmm? I wrote that letter in anger and you know quite well that I regretted it almost immediately.'

He sat down behind her desk, elbows on the arms of the chair, fingers tented together thoughtfully. 'Is that one of the things you were going to tell me last night? That you wanted to stay at the *Woman*?'

'Yes.'

'Then I'm glad I didn't listen to you last night.'

Lesley's temper flared. 'I'll bet you are! As soon as I went to bed with you, you eliminated the complication of my job! Where is it written that a woman can't have both a relationship and a career, Cade? You said a few days ago that if I wanted to stay here, you'd spend more time in Chicago. What happened to that, Cade?'

He didn't answer. Finally, his voice perfectly calm, he said, 'And were you also going to tell me about Melissa?'

Lesley sat down on the high stool. 'So you did take the manuscript. You amaze me, Cade; I thought you'd deny ever seeing it.'

'Thornton will be very unhappy,' Cade said thoughtfully. 'His professional reputation is slipping. I don't know why he neglected to check for a stillborn infant, but he would have got there eventually.'

'How on earth could he have?'

'He had descended to reading old issues of the *Woman*—everything that carried your by-line. Do you realise that in the last four years you've done nine articles on people who lost babies? Everything from miscarriage to crib death. Thornton was becoming suspicious.' He came across the room towards her, suddenly serious. 'Why did you lie to me, Lesley?'

'Why should I tell you anything?' she said bitterly.

'You didn't have any interest in her, or any rights to her.'

'She was my daughter too.'

Lesley wouldn't look at him.

'Yet you wanted to keep that knowledge away from me so much that you let me think you were a con artist—a little liar out to make a dollar.'

'You would have cheapened her memory,' she said finally. 'You would have said something terrible about her—maybe that it was a good thing she died, since no one wanted her anyway. That kind of thing.'

'Do you really think that's how I feel?'

She looked up then, a challenge in her eyes. 'You said that I was unfit to be a mother—that no child deserved a parent like me.'

'I was hurt, Lesley,' he said softly. 'For ten years I've had a sneaking pride that somewhere in this world was a child of mine. Kids in general are one thing, and I don't think much of them. My kid was something else entirely.'

Lesley was silent. She refused to look at him.

'You blasted that pride out of the water. When you told me so coldly that there was no child—that there never had been one—it was actually a physical blow. I couldn't fool myself any longer, I wasn't paying support to a little girl who might even look like me; I'd been conned. That hurt, Lesley.'

There was a long silence, then she said, 'I thought about sending it back. The money that was left, I mean, after I paid for the medical expenses and for the cemetery and everything.' She stared thoughtfully at her clenched hands. 'But I didn't want to account for what I'd spent. And I needed the money right then, which you certainly didn't. So . . .'

'Melissa's money was well-spent, Lesley.' His voice was quiet.

She shredded a tissue into a heap of white fragments. 'Did you read the manuscript?'

'Every word of it,' he admitted cheerfully. 'And I felt

guilty as hell for sneaking downstairs last night and reading it behind your back. I almost hoped that you would wake up and come looking for me.'

'Where is it now?' she asked, very softly.

Cade smiled and shook his head. 'You don't really think I'm going to tell you, do you? It's put away safely until you come to your senses.'

Her control shattered then and she flew across the room, trying to strike at him. He caught at her fists, subduing her after the briefest of struggles, and pushed her down into the chair. Lesley butst into tears.

Cade knelt beside the chair, brushing her tears away with gentle fingers.

'It was bad enough when Mr Thornton humiliated me,' she said, her voice shaking with sobs. 'He kept saying things to trip me up—asking personal questions and making me feel like a tramp . . .'

Cade was suddenly all businessman, not a trace of the lover about him. 'Don't blame Thornton, Lesley. It was his job to ask those questions. He was only doing what I told him to do.'

She plunged on, unhearing. 'And then you—the only thing you cared about was that my baby wasn't named Randall. You'd have paid whatever it cost, just as long as you didn't have to admit to having a child.'

'Yes, I did feel that way, then,' he admitted.

'I was the only one who loved her, the only one who wanted her. And then . . .' she broke off and put a hand over her eyes. 'Then she died.' She looked up at him, a little confused. 'And everybody seemed to think it was a good thing. Even the nurses—oh, they were kind enough, but I could see it in their faces. "Poor baby— what kind of life would she have had? No father, of course, and her mother is only a child herself!" '

Cade massaged the back of her neck, his knuckles trying to rub the tension away.

Lesley pulled away from him. 'Well, I would have been a good mother!' she cried. 'I would have loved her, and cared for her, and raised her right. All the love that

I would have given to her, I bottled up instead, after she died. And when I finally wrote the book, I poured all that love into it.'

'It's obvious how you felt about her, Lesley. It's a good book.'

'Is the compliment supposed to soothe my pride? Cade, I'm not going to let you hide that book away. I want it to be a memorial to Melissa, and to all of the children like her. Your name isn't connected with it, and it's none of your business what I do with it.'

'Is that how you really feel, Lesley? Or are you just taking the opposite stand again? You've been doing that all week, you know—choosing whichever side is opposite to me just for the fun of fighting.' He put a tissue into her hand. 'Dry your tears so you can convince me.'

She dried her eyes, defiantly blew her nose, looked into the mirror inside the closet and patched up her make-up a bit. Then she came back to the desk where he was leaning, arms folded across his chest, and said, 'I want the book published. And it isn't just to aggravate you; I have thought about it, and I decided this morning to let Bob Merrill sell it. That was before I knew you'd stolen it, Cade.'

'Stolen is a strong word, Lesley,' he protested.

'What else would you call it? You certainly didn't have my permission.'

'Are you certain that you won't change your mind again?'

'I'm positive.' She held her chin up defiantly.

He grunted. 'All right. If you're sure, I'll get it out of the hotel vault this afternoon. I owe you a briefcase, by the way. I broke the lock on yours to get the manuscript out.'

Lesley felt deflated. 'You aren't going to argue about it?' she asked curiously.

He turned to look at her, one eyebrow raised. 'Why on earth should I? Why do you think I took it, anyway?'

'To keep it from being published, of course.'

He shook his head. 'The last thing I knew, you were planning to burn it, Lesley. It would be a sin to burn anything as beautiful as *Empty Cradle, Empty Arms*—the cry of a mother for the child she lost.'

'You really do like it?' she whispered.

He nodded. 'Especially the title. It will catch the reader's attention. But I do have one suggestion.'

'I suppose you want me to use a pen name.'

'Only if you choose to. I'm looking forward to seeing shelves and racks full of copies, with you autographing them.'

'Then what do you want?'

He sighed. 'Lesley, give our daughter her real name. Dedicate the book to Melissa Randall.'

She looked up at him in amazement. 'You don't mind if—if people know?'

'I'm ashamed of myself, yes, but not of her. She would have been quite a girl. Our daughter, Lesley—it would have been impossible for her to be ordinary.' He was smiling, just a little.

There was a long silence. 'I would have kept my word, Cade,' she said finally, and her voice was so soft that he had to bend his head to hear. 'If she had lived, she would never have heard your name. But when she died . . . I buried her as Melissa Randall.'

The light in his eyes was almost painful to her. 'Is that why old Thornton had such a time finding her?' he drawled, but there was an undercurrent of joy in his voice. Suddenly serious again, he said, 'I am glad, Lesley. She deserves far more than that, but . . .'

'It was the only thing I could give her, Cade. A name and a little pink granite monument in a tiny cemetery. Not much, was it?'

'And now a book,' he reminded. 'Now that you're not fooling about with the magazine anymore, you'll have time to make it a beautiful memorial to her.'

Fury blazed in Lesley's eyes again. 'How dare you call my job "fooling about"? I love magazines; I've always loved them. I'm good at my job, and whatever you say, Cade Randall, I will not give it up!'

'Too late,' he said calmly. 'Your replacement took over this morning.'

She was crying again, tears of angry frustration this time. 'Why did you take my job away, Cade?'

'Because you were absorbed in it, and it always came first. I want you to be absorbed in me.'

'You want! What about what I want, Cade?'

'I'm listening.' He sat down and gave her his full attention.

'I want to edit the *Woman*. I'll cut back, I really will. With another assistant . . .'

'With another assistant you might be able to spend one week of the month in New York.'

She nodded eagerly.

'Assuming that I could spend a week out here every month, we'd be together half the time. Is that what you want?'

It wasn't, and Lesley was honest enough to admit it to herself. She stared out over the grey city. It was gloomy today; the weak sunshine of early morning had faded under clouds. But she said stubbornly, 'We could make it work, Cade. You said yourself that we could.'

'That was last week. I thought then that it would be enough. Now I know that I want more. I want a relationship that has a chance to grow, and we can't have that with more than a thousand miles between us. I've done a lot of hopping from bed to bed in my life, and I don't want to do that any more. I want to have a love affair with you, Lesley—only you.'

She spun around from the window. 'For how long, Cade? Six months? A year? Five years? What will I have left when it's over? If I give up my job for you, and then you change your mind about this exotic love affair, I'll have memories—nothing more than memories. I will not let a man get in my way, Cade. Never again.'

'I love you, Lesley.' It was quiet, almost without inflection.

'That's not fair, damn it.'

'What's unfair about it? It's true.'

She put her hands on her hips. 'Why don't you give up *Monsieur* and move to Chicago?'

'Lesley, use your common sense.'

'You see? You think that's ridiculous, but you're forcing me to choose between you and my career.'

'You're right. That's exactly what I'm asking. Which is more important to you, Lesley?' The question was quiet, but its implications hung in the air.

There was a long silence. Then Lesley said softly, 'I don't want to be your mistress, Cade.'

He just looked at her, his big brown eyes sad. For what seemed an endless moment, they stood there, the width of the office separating them. Neither of them moved; it seemed they had even stopped breathing.

Then Cade shrugged. He looked suddenly old, and terribly tired. 'I guess that answers my question, doesn't it?' He turned towards the door.

He was leaving. There seemed to be a tight steel band around Lesley's chest; she had to struggle to get a breath. 'I don't want to be just your mistress,' she amended. 'I can't be another Bambi, Cade. I have to work . . .'

He paused, but he didn't turn to face her. 'I'm not asking you to become like Bambi.'

'But without a job or anything, what else can I do? What about your career, Cade? Isn't it important to you?'

'The Randall Group is a job,' he said, and turned around. He leaned against the door and put his hands in his pockets. 'I work forty hours a week. If there is something I can't accomplish in that time, I hire someone to do it. You would be my priority, Lesley.'

'But you're asking me to give up writing, to give up the magazine . . .'

'You can freelance. Write another book.' He flung it out as a challenge.

'But the magazine is in my blood, Cade! I can't give it up!' And I'll die if I give you up, my love, her heart was crying. You're asking me to tear myself in half . . .

Better to be a living half than a dead one. The words rang in her ears. Without the magazine, she would be lonely, lacking a purpose in her life. But without Cade, there would be no life at all.

She put out a hand to him, tears sliding down her cheeks unheeded. 'Whatever you want, Cade,' she said, her voice hardly audible.

His touch was gentle as he scooped the tears from her face. 'Say it, Lesley.'

She buried her face in his shoulder and said, 'I'll do whatever you want, because you are more important to me than anything else in the world.'

'And will you give up everything else? The magazine? The condo? Everything?' There was tension in his voice.

'The condo, too? That's bloody unfair, Cade, and you know it.'

He nodded. 'I know. Will you give it up, Lesley?'

'If you want me to.' It was grudging. 'You're the only man in the world I'd do it for, Cade.'

'Why?' It was a gentle question.

'Because . . .' It was hard to say the words, as if she knew that once said, the fact was more real. Once she told him how important he was to her, Lesley thought, his demands might even increase. 'Because I love you.'

He kissed her gently and then pulled her to her feet. 'As soon as you've removed the tearstains, I'll take you out to lunch.'

'Celebrating?' But she looked at herself in the mirror, sighed at the ravages of emotion, and started once again to repair the damage.

'Among other things. I'd like to tell you my ideas for the Melissa Randall Foundation.'

'What's that?'

'I don't write books, so I had to think of a different way to make sure my daughter is remembered. I think there should be more research into the causes of infant death—don't you?'

'That's marvellous, Cade. I'll contribute my royalties.'

'Don't sign them away too quickly. You may want to take me out for dinner occasionally, you know.' He took her hand and inspected it as if he'd never seen one before. 'And of course we need to talk about your new job.'

'What will I be doing? Giving parties for you or something?' Lesley tried to feel some enthusiasm, but she knew she sounded miserable.

'I was thinking more in terms of giving birth to things,' Cade said thoughtfully. He didn't let go of her hand.

'You've decided to become a family man.' Lesley wasn't sure how she felt about that.

'The possibility is already there, you know,' he said, and kissed each fingertip gently.

Lesley looked down at her flat stomach in sudden shock, as if expecting that she might have blossomed into full-term pregnancy overnight. She probed around the corners of her mind, wondering how she felt about the idea of carrying a child again. Rather neutral, she decided. It might be nice to be pregnant with Cade's child, but it was also scary. What if she lost another baby?

Cade seemed to be reading her mind. He put his arms around her, pulling her back against him, his fingers laced together over her stomach. 'Because Melissa died doesn't mean that we can't have a healthy baby.'

'Do you really want a child, Cade?'

He met her eyes in the little mirror. 'If we have a choice, no. At least not right now,' he amended. 'I would like there to be a child in the world eventually, part of you and part of me. But I'd prefer to have you to myself for a while first. Starting with lunch, since I didn't have breakfast. Are you almost ready?'

Lesley nodded and coloured a little, remembering just why he hadn't had time for breakfast.

'Is Cicero's all right?'

'Fine. But Cade . . .' Her question was tentative. 'If you aren't talking about babies, then what did you mean about me giving birth to things?'

Cade grinned. 'How would you like to be a consultant for the Randall Group? A little lady I know has some great plans for a new magazine, intended for the career woman.'

'My magazine!' Her eyes were like stars. 'Cade, can I have it? Really?'

'Not your magazine,' he warned sternly. 'It will have an editor, and a whole staff of writers, and a business manager. You may tell them what to do, but they will do it.'

'All right,' she agreed breathlessly. 'But I thought . . .'

'And you will not work overtime. If you start putting in more than forty hours a week, I'll fire you.'

'Agreed. I'd rather have that than the *Woman*, anyway.'

'Good. Because you can't have the *Woman*. It's too far away from me, and you could never cut back to a regular work week. You've spoiled your staff for too long.'

'Thank you, Cade.' She flung her arms around him.

He held her a few inches away, and warned, 'Just remember what you told me a few minutes ago, my dear. You cried, but you gave up everything that is precious to you because you said I was more important. Keep the priorities in that order. Because if the day comes that you're too busy with the magazine to have time to play, the magazine dies.'

'But starting up a new title—it's going to take a lot of work.' Her voice was doubtful.

'You will also have a lot of time, and a lot of help. You aren't going to do everything by yourself, and you aren't going to accomplish it all this year.'

'Whatever you say, Cade. Are you going to make me sell the condo?'

'Of course not. We'll need it now and then.'

'I do love it so.'

'More than me?' he growled, teasing.

She shook her head.

'Good. Don't forget it. For your information, by the

way . . .' He put a finger under her chin and tipped her face up. 'I never did sleep with Bambi. In fact, I'm a little hurt that you thought she was my type.'

'Oh,' Lesley said softly. 'I didn't sleep with Jay, either. Ever.'

'I know.'

'How? Because Jay's not that kind?'

'No—because you aren't. There hasn't been anyone at all, has there, Lesley?'

She bit her lip. 'No. Just you.'

'I feel . . . very humble, darling.'

'It's something you won't understand, Cade. Men don't—it's different for them. But once a woman has carried a man's child, part of her always belongs to him. Even if she doesn't ever see him again.'

He shook his head. 'You would have belonged to me, anyway, Lesley. It wasn't Melissa, it was the chemistry between us.'

'You might be right.'

'Of course I am. I knew it as soon as I saw you again. Until then you'd just been an old memory—sometimes pleasant, sometimes not. But then I met that spunky, lovely woman who gave me such a hard time about my loose morals.' He flicked a careless finger across her cheek. 'And I knew I'd made a very bad mistake when I left you in that hotel room ten years ago.'

'I think I was jealous of Bambi,' she murmured.

He gave a whoop of laughter. 'You're tempting me, Miss Allen,' he said, and kissed her hard. 'If I wasn't starving, I'd skip lunch and take you back to bed.'

'The idea has its attractions,' Lesley admitted.

'But I need food.' He turned her around to face the mirror and put the comb back in her hand. 'After we have lunch, let's stop at Tiffany's to look at rings.'

Lesley's comb dropped out of her nerveless hand. She stooped to pick it up and said, breathlessly, 'Did you say—rings?'

'Well, I've never done this before, but it does seem to be the proper thing to do.'

'You don't believe in engagement rings.'

'I don't. I'm only going to put one ring on your finger, and I'm going to do that as soon as it's humanly possible.'

She combed her hair carefully and didn't look at him. 'You don't have to marry me, Cade.'

'Yes, I do.' His voice was grim.

'Having a marriage licence really doesn't mean anything. A piece of paper can't hold a relationship together; it just complicates things.'

He gave her an odd look. 'You've stolen my line. That's exactly why we're getting married.'

'But you don't believe in marriage,' Lesley protested.

'Marriage is an institution that provides a mandatory cooling-off period. That is its chief attraction. Face it, Lesley, it's been less than forty-eight hours since we declared this truce, and you're already tried to kick me out of your life twice.'

'We have fought a lot,' she admitted.

'And we are certainly not going to stop now. You'd be making a dreadful mistake if you got rid of me, so it seems only sensible for me to make sure you'll have a chance to reconsider before you do it.'

'That goes for you too,' she said quietly.

'That's right.' The flippancy died out of his voice, and he was deadly serious as he said, 'I don't want to be without you again, Lesley. Ever again. I want us to belong only to each other—not because it's the moral thing to do, but because it is what we want. I want us to have a love affair that lasts forever and grows stronger with the years. I want to wake up on my ninetieth birthday and find you beside me. Lesley . . .'

She was trembling as she turned to face him. 'Do you mean it? Really?'

'Will you marry me, Lesley?'

All the world was in her eyes as she held out her arms to him.

Here's how to get this special offer from Harlequin! As simple as 1…2…3!

1. Each month, save one Treasury Edition coupon from your favorite Romance or Presents novel.
2. In four months you'll have saved four Treasury Edition coupons (only one coupon per month allowed).
3. Then all you have to do is fill out and return the order form provided, along with the four Treasury Edition coupons required and $1.00 for postage and handling.

Mail to: Harlequin Reader Service

In the U.S.A.	In Canada
P.O. Box 52040	P.O. Box 2800, Postal Station A
Phoenix, AZ 85072-2040	5170 Yonge Street
	Willowdale, Ont. M2N 6J3

RT1-A-2

Please send me my FREE copy of the Janet Dailey Treasury Edition. I have enclosed the four Treasury Edition coupons required and $1.00 for postage and handling along with this order form.

(Please Print)

NAME_____

ADDRESS_____

CITY_____

STATE/PROV._____ ZIP/POSTAL CODE_____

SIGNATURE_____

This offer is limited to one order per household.

SUPPLIES LIMITED

This special Janet Dailey offer expires January 1986.

You're invited to accept 4 books and a surprise gift Free!

Acceptance Card

Mail to: **Harlequin Reader Service®**

In the U.S.
2504 West Southern Ave.
Tempe, AZ 85282

In Canada
P.O. Box 2800, Postal Station A
5170 Yonge Street
Willowdale, Ontario M2N 6J3

YES! Please send me 4 free Harlequin Presents® novels and my free surprise gift. Then send me 8 brand new novels every month as they come off the presses. Bill me at the low price of $1.75 each ($1.95 in Canada)—an 11% saving off the retail price. There are no shipping, handling or other hidden costs. There is no minimum number of books I must purchase. I can always return a shipment and cancel at any time. Even if I never buy another book from Harlequin, the 4 free novels and the surprise gift are mine to keep forever.

108 BPP-BPGE

Name _____ (PLEASE PRINT)

Address _____ Apt. No. _____

City _____ State/Prov. _____ Zip/Postal Code _____

This offer is limited to one order per household and not valid to present subscribers. Price is subject to change.

ACP-SUB-1

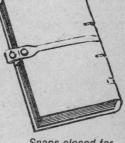